Reckoning

RECKONING

A.S. Penne

TURNSTONE PRESS

Reckoning
copyright © A.S. Penne 2008

Turnstone Press
Artspace Building
018-100 Arthur Street
Winnipeg, MB
R3B 1H3 Canada
www.TurnstonePress.com

Turnstone Press gratefully acknowledges the assistance of the Canada Council for the Arts, the Manitoba Arts Council, the Government of Canada through the Book Publishing Industry Development Program, and the Government of Manitoba through the Department of Culture, Heritage and Tourism, Arts Branch, for our publishing activities.

These stories are works of fiction. Names, characters, places and incidents are either the product of the author's imagination or are used fictitiously, and any resemblance to actual persons living or dead, events or locales, is entirely coincidental.

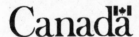 

Cover design: Doowah Design
Interior design: Sharon Caseburg
Printed and bound in Canada by Friesens for Turnstone Press

Library and Archives Canada Cataloguing in Publication

Penne, A. S. (Anthea S.), 1951-
    Reckoning / A.S. Penne.

ISBN 978-0-88801-337-8

    I. Title.

PS8631.E553R42 2008   C813'.6   C2008-901425-1

For John and Joy, in appreciation of their company on the road.

Contents

A Different Kind of Wanting

Funny how you can understand life only by looking at it backwards. Kind of like those skill tests where the first instruction tells you to read it all before you do anything, but then the very next line says to write your name in the upper right-hand corner of the paper and so you go ahead and do it, forgetting about that first instruction. You just go right ahead and write your name without thinking about what you're doing. And then when you get to the end—after about twenty instructions—the last line says something like, "*Now that you've finished reading everything, follow the directions of numbers six and eight only.*" But I was always so goal-oriented that by the time I reached the end, every last detail was completed and I'd have to erase the ones I shouldn't have done. And the only thing I could do then was groan and shake my head in regret that I'd screwed up. Again.

It must've been 1955, '56 maybe. I bought a new station wagon for Joanne to haul the kids around in. It was a two-tone Buick, white on baby blue, and that summer we took it camping. Packed it to the ceiling and drove up the Fraser Canyon in 110-degree weather, snaking along the old two-lane highway with sun glaring off the roofs of cars ahead like a steel convoy. It was a long drive, me pushing to drive straight through and Joanne and the kids and dog wanting to stop for a drink and some shade every hour. After five hours in the stifling car, even Jay was quiet, his six-year-old face flushed and hair damp. Just outside Kamloops, I turned off the highway and we bumped down an old dirt road into the bush. Jay sat forward expectantly, his hands gripping the back of my seat.

"Where are we going, Dad? Are we exploring? Does this go somewhere?"

I could feel his hot child's breath on my neck. In the rear-view mirror I saw his eyes, big as angels' wings, and the contrast of his brother slumped against the rear door. Eleven-year-old Grant was deep in a comic book, trying to hold it steady against Jay's fidgeting. "Sit still, wouldja!" His sneer surfaced over the top of the comic, but Jay didn't hear him.

"Aw, neat!" Jay sighed when the lake came into sight. "Can we go swimming? Didja bring the diving mask, Mom?"

It was midnight before Jay got to sleep that night. By 5:00 he was already awake.

After breakfast we left Joanne at the campsite with a good book. The three of us took the fly gear and hiked along the bank of a small river until the rock face of a canyon halted us. Jay couldn't stop talking as we sat on the pebbled beach to put on waders.

"Is this where the fish are, Dad? Are we going to catch one for dinner? I want to catch a salmon. Will you help me catch the salmon?"

"You're such a twit." Grant's mutter was low enough that I pretended not to hear. I understood his annoyance at having to share this favourite hobby with Jay, but I figured the time had come for one activity we could all do together. Sometimes you want a thing so much you'll do almost anything to achieve it.

2

"No salmon here, Jay." I smiled at him. "How 'bout a nice. rainbow?"

He stopped struggling with the oversized waders and turned his big eyes on me. "With the pot of gold?"

His innocence made me wince. I knew if Joanne were here she'd laugh with him, encourage his imagination. But I was discomforted by the thought that he was too young, that I was hurrying him into something too soon. So I raised my eyebrows and shrugged at him: "You never know, eh?"

Jay's hand buried into mine as I led him along the riverbed, staying close to the cliff and avoiding the swirling centres of waters where a minor slip could pull him under, carry his small body away like so much litter. Grant plodded ahead, making for a pool we'd fished the year before. He found a ledge beneath a grove of heavy aspens and left the gear there, wading back out to the rocks. I watched him for a moment, saw how he found his position in the flow of water, bracing his feet against the riverbed, then throwing his line at a downstream pool where the streaks of shadows and sunlight played tricks on the surface. I felt that quickening in my gut, the homogenous mix of pleasure and sentiment that always rose whenever I watched him work a stream.

The mayflies were out so I tied one on a line while Jay splashed noisily along the shore. He looked up in surprise when I called him, as if he'd forgotten where he was or why we were there. He stood at the edge of those dark, icy waters, staring back at me as if I were some kind of vision.

I held the rod out to him, leaning over his sandy head and covering his small hands with my big ones while he stood between my legs. I showed him how to brace his feet and how to move his wrist and arm, backwards and forwards in a movement that could, if he let it, change his life. I told him to close his eyes and imagine a beam of light streaming from his fingertips like one of his heroes on those Saturday morning cartoons. And as the line hummed through the air, I took my hands off the rod to let him feel it on his own.

Jay struggled to find the rhythm and twice I had to cut the fly and retie it when it caught on a deadhead. Again and again we launched the line, but Jay's quick, jerky movements continued to defeat him. It reminded me of the uncoordinated way he ran, bony knees bent in a sudden attempt to sprint while his arms hung back, unmoving and unmoveable. Spastic, Grant always said.

I led him away from the curve of the beach then, out to the middle of a shallow pool where the water was slow—too unprotected to catch anything, including a fish, but where he could have some room and maybe some success. I helped him send out the line, then showed him how to give it some slack and pull it back, reeling it in when it drifted too far. He was loosening up, making small progress when Grant appeared.

"They're biting over there, Dad." He held up two good-sized cutthroats.

"Hey—well done! What're you using?" I let go of Jay's rod and waded towards Grant.

"I think I'm going to try a gnat. They're swarming over there."

I reached for the fish, but when I turned to show them to Jay, I dropped them quickly. Jay was teetering forward, the tip of the rod bent nearly double as it arced toward the pool. The line quivered, disappearing at a taut angle, the fly not even visible in the distance.

Back at the campsite, I tried to figure out what had happened. "I guess he caught it on a deadhead—might've been a bite, who knows?—and he kept pulling out more and more line to free it and then he was in the water." I shook my head and looked at Joanne.

She had a worried frown on her face when she spoke. "Maybe you should back off, Frank," was what she said.

"Fishing?"

She shrugged and then she drew a deep breath, as though in pain. I put my arm around her and we watched the sunset. The day had been long, but it was good to be out in the bush again, Joanne's head on my shoulder and the kids asleep in the tent. I found myself thinking that this was all I really wanted, some peace and quiet like this. Everything would work itself out, I figured. Somehow.

Jay wanted to hike with Joanne the next day so Grant and I went out alone. We went back to the same spot and tried the black gnat but the fish weren't biting. After a few hours of no action, we stopped to eat. Grant and I sat in companionable silence, neither of us real talkers, and listened to the sounds of the water and the birds.

"Is there something wrong with Jay, Dad?"

The question rose like a prize tug on the line. I stared at him in shock. "What makes you say that?"

Grant picked up a rock and lobbed it at the pool in front of us. "He doesn't like the same things as us."

"Lots of people like things others don't."

"Yeah, but he's different."

"How is he different?"

Grant shrugged and his mouth twisted into a wry grin. "It's kinda weird to like hiking and berry picking more than fishing."

"You and I think so, maybe. I guess it's different for him."

He turned to stare inquiringly, his steely eyes boring like drills. "Yeah. That's what I mean."

I thought of that skinny little kid with Joanne and tried to imagine him here with us, but I could only see the way he'd been yesterday, arms crossed across his shivering chest, a stream of snot drooling over his lips as he hunched his way out of the dark water.

"I don't know, Grant." I shook my head and looked downstream. "That's just the way it is, I guess."

The water made a loud roar as it rushed through the channel in front of us, but I could still hear the disgusted click of Grant's tongue over it.

I rented a boat to take out on the lake. Jay's excitement at this new possibility was so uncontainable that he insisted on waiting in the boat until we were ready to go out. Joanne took him his hot chocolate and he sat there, eyes watching my every move and willing me to hurry. His was a different kind of wanting, I guess; one I couldn't fathom.

Jay didn't have what it took to go fishing with us. He was too rest-less to be confined that way for hours, holding a dead line and waiting,

waiting. He sank lower and lower into his chin-hugging life jacket, as if by doing that he could slip out and down through the bottom of the boat, get away. After half an hour he was fidgeting so much that the rocking of the boat caused a small wake and Grant was itching to slug him. Maybe that's why, when Grant felt a small tug, he yanked so hard on his line that the trout came flipping through the air and broadsided Jay's head.

Jay had never seen a live fish up close, except at the aquarium. The look of shock on his face turned to one of revolt when he saw the flopping body on his lap and heard Grant yelling, "Hit it! Hit it, dummy!" I wedged my rod into the slot of my seat and reached, half squatting and half leaning for the line, but in that moment Jay stood up. He twisted himself away from the gasping, thumping life on the floor of the boat and lost his balance. In the time it took for me to grab for the loose ties of his life jacket, Jay was overboard. When his head broke the lake's surface, I saw the explosion of hysteria in his eyes. He wouldn't listen when I told him to stay calm so I yelled at him.

"You're not drowning, for Chrissakes—give me your hand!" But the kid kept on blubbering and thrashing, blubbering and thrashing until his life jacket had him in a stranglehold and he couldn't move his arms.

It was Grant who turned the prow of the boat, reaching over its edge with the oar so Jay could feel the solidness of the wood beneath him. Grant pulled his brother alongside while I watched those sneakered feet pushing desperately at the water.

When I knelt over the gunwales to grip beneath his arms, Jay's wet hair nuzzled my cheek. I heaved his waterlogged body onto my shoulder and sat back, pulling him with me and feeling the slow pathways of water dribbling down my chest. He hadn't felt that little since he was born.

But the stale smell of lake water on him made me push him away from my face. The dog was barking and when I looked up, the bloody thing was swimming towards us. Joanne was frantic, wading into the water at the lake's edge and looking like she wanted to follow the damned dog. She was holding up her trouser legs to keep them from getting wet and her red lips were moving, saying something I couldn't read. I waved to signal it was okay but I knew she wouldn't believe me and all of a sudden I was angry. "Call the goddamned dog back, Joanne! Jesus Christ, stop worrying!" Jay was pale and shivering between my legs, his doleful eyes afraid of what he'd done.

Grant's sighs drowned out the sound of the rhythmic drip from the oars as I rowed. Joanne's anxiety floated across the stillness: "Where's Jay? Is he all right?" I hunched over the oars and didn't bother to answer. Grant cupped his hands around his mouth and called out, "We're bringing him in!" I wanted to unload the kid, forget about his misery and mine. If I could just get away from him, I could calm down, stop hating myself for thinking the incident was so important. For thinking that taking him had been such a waste of time.

What I wanted was for everything to be different. What I wanted was to lose this troubling feeling that Jay was impossible.

That night in front of the fire I tried to include Jay in the talk about going out next day. I'd seen a likely spot around the curve of the lake and Grant wanted to try his new fly, but Jay seemed uninterested. He sat quietly off in his own world and didn't complain when Grant shoved him off the marshmallow roasting rock. I assumed he'd had enough of this fishing business and he'd wait another year before he joined in again. I began to think that would be best for all of us, so I was surprised when he appeared at the side of the boat next morning. He didn't say a word, just put on his life jacket and hopped in, waiting.

Grant stopped for a minute and looked at me. "Dad?" he asked, wanting me to react.

"Get in, Grant," I snapped.

It was dark and bone-chilling cold at 5:30 in the morning. Slices of early light cut ridges of shadow on the mountains as we rowed out to the middle of the lake, and the plup of the oars dipping and lifting out of the black water echoed off the treed shoreline.

None of us spoke. I thought that was because even the boys could feel the magic of the stillness around us. That was what I had brought my sons there for, to feel the wilderness, the outdoor life we forget about during those long electric winters buried by noise in the city. I wanted them to hear the empty silence, to carry it with them always. And then suddenly someone was whimpering. Jay.

"I have to pee, Dad! I forgot to go pee before I left!"

Grant laughed, a vicious, hollow sound carried low into the mists. "Pee over the edge."

"I can't reach."

"What do you mean, son?"

"It won't go over the edge, it's below the edge."

"Well, stand up then, boy."

"NOOOO!" a loud, mournful howl into the darkness, tears and clutching at his crotch like he was going to split open with the pain.

It didn't matter what I tried to say to him then. Jay wouldn't take the risk of being in that black water again. We had to go back to shore and unload him, bawling and mewing, into his mother's arms. I left him there, avoided her freezing blue eyes by concentrating on turning the boat and rowing away.

Grant's voice came out of the shadows. "What was Mom mad about, Dad?"

I was glad there wasn't enough light yet for him to see me clearly. "Why did you think she was mad?"

"She looked at you funny."

"I didn't notice." And I pretended I couldn't hear the empty crying through the darkness. Sound carries a long way on water.

I could see Jay running back and forth on the shore when we turned the point later. He was shouting and waving and for a minute I worried that something had happened to Joanne, but then she appeared, walking toward the edge where Jay was leaping about like a frog. I saw her lean down and put her hands on his shoulders, as if to calm him, but Jay wriggled past her and bounced along the beach, waiting for us.

"I got a fish! I got a fish!" he was yelling from between his cupped hands. As we got closer I could see Joanne holding up his rod and pointing to a miniscule flash of silver dangling at the end of its line.

"Hey, look at that!" I called back, a warm pleasure rising in my throat.

"It's too small, Dad. He shouldn't have kept it!" The jealousy in Grant's voice was palpable.

I put my hand over his on the oars. "Don't tell him that, Grant," I warned him. "Just leave it be this time."

Jay held the tiny fingerling stretched between his thumbs and fore-fingers and I marvelled at the possibility of catching anything quite so small, but I listened with interest to his disjointed description of the catch.

"... and then he tried to get off the line and he twisted and jumped out of the water—like this—" Jay's hand mimicked the action of a much larger fish struggling for freedom and I smiled and patted his shoulder.

"How about a picture of you with your first catch?"

Joanne posed with Jay, and then with both the boys. She stood with an arm around each of their waists, all three of them grinning at the success of the day.

But when Grant and I invited Jay to clean his fish with ours, he re-fused, his smooth brow bunching into concerned wrinkles. "No, Dad. I'm not going to split him open and take everything out of him. He's my fish and I'm going to keep him, not eat him."

Grant turned towards Jay with a look of pure disbelief. Unable to contain himself any longer, he spat his disgust.

"You're such a dipstick, Jay! The fish is dead—it's useless! It's too small to eat and you can't keep it unless you freeze it so what's the point?" I looked at him, too stunned to stop his tirade. From a distance I could see Joanne waving at me frantically. Jay's eyes turned as dark as the water and he started to walk away.

"It's a puny, stinking excuse for a fish!" Grant yelled at him.

My hand went out, its back contacting the side of Grant's head without hesitation, without thought, knocking him to the ground as though he were some kind of floundering life at the end of my rod and the only instinct I had was to beat it senseless.

It's one of those incidents that niggles at my memory like a sliver in the web between thumb and forefinger. I keep wondering how things came to be so hard between my boys and me. How I could've been better at encouraging them, at helping them be friends, maybe. It began to seem then that things had been so much easier before Jay came into our lives and that he'd somehow stirred up all the muck. Like some kind of bottom-feeder, sweeping his tail back and forth over all that silt beneath the dark waters.

It was another twenty-five years before I got the phone call that changed it all.

"This is Corporal Jessen from the Kamloops RCMP," a deep voice said. "I'm calling for a Mr. Frank Bisworth."

If I'd known it would end so badly, I would never have been so hard on him. On any of us.

A tourist at the public campsite on the lake found him. A tourist standing on the public dock looking down into the lake. And a young officer—not much older than Jay would've been—pulled what was left of his body from those unforgiving waters. I wanted to go identify him, make sure it was Jay, but they wouldn't let me. Said there wasn't much of him left to identify—he'd been in the water at least three weeks. Cold water. Dark water. I kept seeing that little boy's sandy hair streaming around his head and remembering how scared he'd been in that lake.

On my desk is a framed copy of that picture of Jay's first fish. Joanne calls it "The Invisible Catch" because you can't really see the fish in the graininess of the shot. Unless you know where to look.

But Jay's face is so visible that sometimes I want to reach out, touch him back to life.

And now that the only thing I can do about it is remember, I keep thinking how familiar this feeling is. This wanting to erase and wishing I could change my responses.

Now that you're finished ...

It's a part of my life I'd like to do over again, do right.

... go back ...

Because Jay was so proud of that stupid fish. As if that was all he really wanted.

How to Take a Lover

When he calls you up and reminds you who he is, sound pleased to hear from him. Of course you remember that softball game, though it's his bulging arm muscles you recall, not the leg-bloodying slide at third base that he'd like you to see. Laugh flirtatiously at his innocuous jokes and puns, as if you've never been more entertained in your life, and try not to worry about the amount of time you're spending on this call when you should be proofreading a manuscript or taking your four-year-old son to the park, the son you don't spend enough of any kind of time with—especially quality time—these days.

If he doesn't ask you out right away, assume that he is probably the shy type and he has to work himself up to it. Be glad for the reprieve of a few extra days, maybe a whole week, to catch up on your work. That way, if he takes the big step, you can devote your whole attention to him.

When he calls next, don't tell him you were actually asleep because of the overtime you've been working, trying to meet the publisher's deadline. Tell him you'd love to have dinner with him next week, and yes, you suppose you could have it at your place since he has roommates. Tell him also, with an inexplicable mixture of shame and pride, that you have a young son who lives with you. Listen for his surprise, his almost-reticence, and when you don't hear it, congratulate yourself on having finally met a man who likes kids. Or seems to.

As the evening approaches, don't panic that you haven't the time to cook anything special or clean the house. Take all the manuscripts off the small dining table and put them in separate piles on your bedroom floor with the assumption he won't be seeing that room—surely he won't stay the night this first time? Think about the last time you spent the night with a man—almost a year now—and then put away those shivers of anticipation. Or premonition. Ask yourself if you really want to be intimate with a man again, but don't take the question too seriously. Questions like that have a way of becoming fuel for fantasies.

Draw a steamy bath and perfume it with lavender, trying to wake yourself up and relax at the same time. Remember that he expects only to enjoy your company, not to spend the rest of his life with you. At this point.

Find something appropriate—not too comfortable or too inviting—to wear. Remind yourself that you don't want to come on to him, though you do want to impress him. Keep in mind that he may not turn out to be the man of your dreams.

Don't place too much importance on the fact that the wine he brings is the bubbling pink stuff you drank in high school. Remember that you developed a taste for fine wine only after exposure by your ex-husband, the Concordia graduate. Try not to compare a wine connoisseur to a social worker and do not squirm when he tries to impress you by saying, "Clinton makes such a poultry effort to be ethical." Tell him you're not a big drinker when he notices your still-full wineglass, offering it to him if he looks disappointed. Smile graciously when he tells you that he hates to see good wine go to waste.

At 11:00, try to stifle your yawns by remembering that no one else goes to bed this early on weekends. Let his Valentino eyes swim over you, engulf you. Tell yourself that another night of insufficient sleep won't make a difference, but that his presence in your life may.

At 2:00 a.m. remind him of the child asleep in the next room. Point out, because he's obviously unaware, that kids do not observe clocks and that your son will be awake by 7:00 a.m. Tell him you need to say goodnight. At the door, when he asks if it would be all right to kiss you good night, give him an all-out hug. Don't hesitate to tell him you had a wonderful time.

Feel pleased when your girlfriend—the one who introduced you to this man—says that he hasn't dated for several years because of a previously disastrous affair. Flatter yourself that you are special, you are different; he will not have a hard time with you because you know how to love a man. Truly. Address the issue of whether you can love this particular man later.

When you first make love, ignore the fact that it was you who promoted the idea and that he doesn't seem comfortable being naked beside you. Don't let his apparent reticence unnerve you, hurry you through the act. Remember that he can be taught the skills of foreplay later. Now it is more important not to overwhelm him with your orgasm. You don't want him to think you're loose. Or horny. Assume that once you know each other better, things will change.

In fact, many things change. Your son, once enamoured with your new friend, will begin to feel ousted as more and more of your time is consumed by the man who now claims the side of the bed that before was your son's. Assuage everyone's hurt feelings. Tell the real child that you will schedule regular times to play with him so he won't feel forgotten when you leave him with a babysitter and tell the other child—speaking both parentally and financially—that you really can't afford to go out so often. When he pouts, pour yourself a good shot of Southern Comfort and have another long, hot bath.

If he curls his lip the first time you suggest making love during your period, understand that this man-child isn't what he pretends. When, months later, he concedes that a week-long hiking trip during your period would be okay because you are "discreet about that sort of thing," try not to sneer back at him. Though you've already known him a year, be patient with him. He's only a man.

You meet his family and are welcomed like a celebrity. Carry this suggestion of belonging as you move into their sphere. At your lover's suggestion, encourage your son to call his mother Gramma, even though the older woman fusses whenever he stands too near her glitzy knickknacks. Later, when Gramma and the sisters discuss fashion, stifle the laughter that rises when they ask, "Are you summer or winter?" Understand that the question is serious. Try not to notice where the door is, that the other brother never comes to these family gatherings, and that the mother talks like one of those high-voiced baby dolls with a string in her back.

On the way home from family dinners, plead fatigue in order to minimize conversation. In fact, try to avoid speaking at all and thus the temptation to criticize. Instead, make a face at the driver of the car in the lane beside you, and yawn at his comments in apparently complacent agreement. The next time a family dinner comes up, excuse yourself by remembering a promise to take your child to the movies or to go out with a girlfriend, the one who set you up with this man.

But don't tell her how hopeless you're feeling. Don't admit it to anybody yet, not even yourself. Keep working at building the relationship; keep convincing yourself that things will improve. Believe that eventually he will enjoy doing things with your child, that he will inquire about both of your days and not talk only about his during and after the dinner he never cooks or cleans up from, that he will learn how to maintain a household and a house instead of relying on band-aid repairs or your savings account for major problems. Believe all this and ignore the thought that you are a stupid fool.

And when he asks you to marry him, don't falter. Don't tell him you want to think about it, despite the little voice in your head screaming, "No! No!" Ignore your intuition and tell yourself that your son needs a father, you need a mate, and that everything will work out. That even the sex might improve when you've committed your lives to each other.

Feel pleased, as if you have made the right choice, when both your parents are thrilled by the announcement. Take it as high praise when your father says that your lover's strong handshake and direct eye contact are the traits of a real man. Don't tell your father that the real man doesn't know how to balance a bank statement or repair a leaky pipe; that his favourite TV show is *Star Trek*. Don't tell your father how you lay awake one night crying, wishing you could move back home and start all over again. He would laugh at you and you don't need that.

When you tell your sister that you think you're pregnant—you know you are, you just don't want to admit it—avoid seeing how her eyes take on that blank look, a look that means, "Oh God, here we go again." Allow yourself to be concerned with the many small details of a big wedding and—though your parents tell you not to worry about the expense—try to ignore the memory that your sister's wedding was a family-only affair.

And when your introverted brother is overly genial at the wedding reception, pumping your new husband's hand and acting as if this was the best moment in recent family history, try to avoid remembering that he himself is twice divorced. That it can happen again.

Take lots of photos, watch your father get drunk, tell your tear-stained son he is still your prince despite the fact that his new aunt has spilled wine all over his pants so that it looks like he peed himself. Go home exhausted, accompanied by a groom who has expectations that this night, more than the first one spent together, will go down in history—or at least in memory.

When the pregnancy ends in miscarriage and your son becomes this man's only opportunity to be a father, try not to notice his abrupt coldness towards the child. Ignore how he chooses to mow the lawn, a chore he will normally avoid, rather than play catch with your son. Look out the window and see how he hurls the mower around corners, viciously, as a way of expressing his loss. Months later, when it is apparent that neither his resentment nor your anger can be cured without outside help, admit that the love is fading. Stay with it until he categorically refuses to see a counsellor, then make the decision—slowly, painfully—to dissolve this second marriage. Notice that he doesn't argue when you announce your intention to leave.

Believe that you've learned your lesson and that you won't make the same mistake a third time. Buy a self-help book on filing for divorce and avoid a horrendous legal bill. Spend six months readjusting to life and, when the Decree Absolute becomes final, wonder why you don't feel more relief, more freedom from that Supreme Court certificate. Go to a framing store and choose an all-black frame for the decree. Hang it next to your equally unrelieving university degree.

And when the next phone call comes, from him or from any of the other men who want to know why you won't make more time for them, mention that you've decided to come out. Hope that by saying this, you'll scare them off or at least force them to re-evaluate what they want from you. If that doesn't work, point out that if they'd like to sleep with a lesbian, you know lots of other gay women. Tell them, in fact, that most of your friends are gay. Hang the receiver up softly, avoid the temptation to drop it from shoulder height.

Summer About to Happen

George and me in the front seat of the car, Dawne and some other guy in the back. Guitar twangs and a cowboy crooner on the car radio, and behind all that a lot of hushed noise from the rear seat. George leans against the driver's door and I'm sitting back against the passenger side and every so often George passes me a mickey and I take it but only wet my lips on the burn of liquor, not wanting to barf like the last time I drank hard stuff. When I hand it back to him, our rings click against each other, and in the faint moonlight I can see the chips of diamonds on his finger. His is the kind of ring that movie gangsters wear, a flashy black surface with the diamonds set in the shape of his initial. Mine is an old signet ring, gold, with a family crest that goes back to whenever.

It makes me think about home and school and how glad I am it's over for another year. But then I picture my English teacher for some reason and I start to giggle. Sitting here with our feet tangled together like blackberry vines over the hump in the centre, we're in what Mr. Morrison would call Theatre of the Parked Car. It's got the setting, the characters, the tension, even a little bit of action, at least in the back. I look across at George and see him staring at me with a question on his face and I think how I'd like to tangle more than my legs around this guy. But I'm not much like Dawne and I guess he's not like that other guy back there either or we'd be making the same kind of noises they are. I feel like something's going to happen and part of me wants it to hurry up and be over with but part of me is completely freaked by it.

The wet sound of lips releasing flesh comes like some kind of loudspeaker announcement behind us. George takes one last slug out of his bottle, then reaches for my hand.

"C'mon," he says as he opens the door. I slide across the bench seat towards him and out into the cool night air and stand there, hugging my bare arms. He tucks his black T-shirt into his tight black jeans, then slips a comb out of the back pocket and I turn away so as not to have to watch him run it through his oiled hair. I think of all the private-school boys back home, their soft curls and corduroy pants, and know they'd sneer at my being here with a greaser.

I'm sixteen, seventeen next fall when I go back to school for my final year, and George could be thirty for all I know. He doesn't talk much—only nodded when we were introduced—but I don't mind, I guess. I mean, the guys I'm used to are so slick with their lines that there's something to be said for the way George doesn't seem to want to bother. As long as he doesn't think I'm just a kid.

"You wanna swim?" he asks and I look at him, thinking, Okay—here it comes. And then I wonder how I could've been so naïve as to think he was different.

"I don't have a suit on," I tell him. Expecting the argument, expecting the skinny-dip suggestion.

But no. He shrugs and says, "Okay." He starts walking towards the water, stops and turns to look back at me. "You wanna have a fire?"

"No marshmallows," I say.

George looks away. Then he grins and says, "I'll go get some."

The thought of him leaving me here alone while Dawne and

Whatsisname are going at it in the car is almost as bad as the idea of a skinny dip. "No, I will."

George comes back and stands in front of me. "C'mon, then." Holding out his hand.

I stare at it and then stare at him and he has such a gentle face that I put my hand in his.

I used to come here in the summer when I was little, before my grandfather left a cigar burning in the ashtray and the family cabin burned down. But I remember Sunnyside Market, the old country store in the middle of the park, and how my mother used to give me a nickel after dinner sometimes, tell my brother to take me there for a Popsicle. Cal would do it semi-reluctantly—he wasn't old enough to stay out late by himself so I was the excuse for him to go hang out at the store.

We'd walk across the dried meadow to the old wooden building and then he'd send me up the stairs while he lingered at the bottom, eyeing the girls with backcombed hair and spiked heels huddled in small groups, smoking and chewing gum, waiting. From the top of the steep flight of stairs I'd see him step up to one or the other of the girls with too-black eyes, whip his rat-tail comb out of his back jean pocket and slick back his hair in that first step of the 1950s courting ritual.

Then I'd push my way through the whining screen door of the old store, hearing the bell that announced my presence and letting the door swing shut with a slap. I'd spend an agonizing ten minutes digging through the supply of Popsicles until I found something special, root beer or cherry if I was really lucky. Then I'd take my choice to the worn wooden counter, feeling the rough floor under my bare feet while the old man on the other side pushed the heavy round buttons of the ancient cash register.

And when I came back out the screen door, the dusk would be settled and the moths swirling around the light above the door so I didn't wait but went straight down the stairs. I'd linger in the shadows, tearing the paper wrap from the Popsicle to let my brother know I was there, peering into the darkness where the silhouette of his head appeared like a huge shadow on the white of some girl's cardigan. Then he'd tip his head into the halo of light and point towards home so I'd start off by myself, moving slowly so he could catch up to me and I didn't mind because by then my mouth would be full of sweetness and I was content.

When George and I set off across that same meadow, I was remembering being a little girl walking that route with my brother. Remembering how it had felt to be in Cal's company with his mind somewhere else, so that when I asked him a question I often got no answer. At first I wondered if that's what George's quietness was all about. Except this time my hand was being held so I had something else besides the silence to concentrate on.

Those childhood summers brought me back here. They had seemed to be full of a lightness I'd lost; a time when my parents had been happy too. Maybe I'm trying to recapture that invisible loss, I don't know. But when my father brought up the idea of working in his law firm for the second summer in a row, I thought about the articling students who liked to stand at my desk and give me orders so they could stare down my blouse.

"So you're the boss's kid," they'd wink at me. "Where do you go to school?" As if they gave a shit. It made me antsy, pretending to be sweet and innocent around dorks who thought they were so special because one day they were going to be Somebody.

I told my dad that I thought it would be better if I found my own job this summer. And then I told him about the ad I'd seen in the paper for berry pickers in Yarrow.

But I had to steer him away from arguing that his daughter would be a labourer so I added, "I don't think I should always let you find me a job."

He liked that. Said it showed initiative. Mom was the next problem.

"You're only sixteen!" she shrieked. As if I'd forgotten my age.

"What if Dawne came with me?" I suggested.

Dawne's older than me. She left home—got thrown out or ran away from life in a small logging town—two years ago and came to

Vancouver to live with her aunt and uncle, our neighbours. But it didn't work for her there, either, and she dropped out of school last year. Mom says Dawne's very worldly, and she says that in a way I understand to be negative, but I know she likes her. Dawne's gone out of her way to make friends with my parents so they trust her.

Dawne's not a pretty girl. She is overweight and dyes her hair a banana yellow that I really hate. Maybe she does it because she hopes it'll make her pretty. Maybe she lets boys do things to her so they'll like her better. I don't know. But at least she can talk about stuff like sex that my other friends can't discuss for some reason. Plus she's been like a second mom to me, teaching me how to make coffee and Caesar salad and other grown-up stuff. And one night she held my head when I drank too much rye and was sick all over someone's mother's prize rose bushes. That was the night she nicknamed me Barf.

Then in May this year she got fired from her job at the Dairy Queen, which is a whole other story, so the timing was right to suggest coming up here. This would be my last summer before graduating; my last summer as a kid. I wanted to remember it.

We headed east up the Fraser Valley, past the industrial warehouses and the car lots of Surrey, over the muddied river swollen by the spring run-off. We went through the Bible belt of Langley and Abbotsford where the pastoral fields and strong manure smells of farms dotted with black and white cows lulled us into thinking that this summer would be a long and easy one.

The berry farmer met us at the bus station and drove us back to his property. He took us to a bunkhouse at the edge of the fields, a small hut with wood floors and a dollhouse-sized kitchenette that we shared with two others. The rental for our housing was to come out of our weekly paycheques and since the hourly wage was the minimum allowed by the province, there wouldn't be any money made this summer. But I weighed that against the total freedom I would have—from my parents, from the expectations of long-time friends, from all the city hustle and bustle—and this was better. When the farmer left us to settle in, I stepped outside the door and sat on the bunkhouse stoop to

look across the fields of raspberry canes, searching the horizon for a
sight to fix on. The night air danced down around me, steam rising off
the rich soil under the rays of the sinking sun, and the restlessness in
my gut reared up again.

"Hey," I called over my shoulder to the other three inside. "Anyone
want to go for a walk?"

They came to stand in the doorway behind me and we looked out
over the long rows of red berries. I stood and stretched, moving down
the stairs. Someone closed the door on our small cabin with its patched
roof and mildewed floors, and we started towards the nearby town.
And all of us, me and Dawne and Jackie and Ruby, two Okanagan girls
working their way towards the Big City, felt the anticipation of summer
about to happen.

The farmer's son drives the truck of empty slats into the yard each
morning at 7:00. He stands on the deck of the open truck, sunbleached
hair and weathered skin like an ad for instant machismo, and delivers
a quick sales pitch.

"Yesterday"—or the day before or last week or some other time—
"Nancy turned in eighteen slats." His tone underlines the word "eighteen," makes the number seem as monumental as Miss August's bust
measurement, and then his blue eyes blanket Nancy. The rest of us turn
and watch her blush at his attention. Most of the berry pickers are female and what we are doing is not so much listening to the young buck
in front of us as staring hungrily. Even I, probably the only virgin in the
place, like to imagine this early-morning Adonis in some other setting.
Somewhere more bedroomy with candlelight and music, for starters.

"Putting him in front of us first thing in the morning is a bloody
inspiration," Dawne snickers beside me.

By the time we hit the endless rows of raspberry canes, I feel something powerful racing through my veins, something hot and driving
and uncomfortable with insistence.

But it's hard to stay that driven under a 103-degree sun. We ache,
complain non-stop and vow to quit daily. And each night when the sun
drifts over the field outside our door, we sit outside with cold drinks

and lean against each other, our aching muscles freshly showered. A gradual restlessness overtakes us and once more we feel the lure of whatever is beckoning out there, as though our real lives were waiting just around the corner. Eventually one of us stands, staring towards the distance and the small town of Yarrow, and, without any invitation, the other three drain their drinks and stand too, and we stroll towards those sparkling lights as though drawn by them.

Ruby and Jackie are practically related because Jackie is engaged to Ruby's brother. Jackie is supposed to be keeping an eye on Ruby because her mother thinks she's too young to be away from home. But one day, after reading the almost-daily love letter from Steve, Jackie announces she's going home.

"He misses me," she says, holding up the letter as proof.

I nod at her, wondering at, or maybe envious of, the ring-sized announcement. But then I look over at Dawne who is taking a drag from her cigarette and staring questioningly at Jackie through the smoke.

"I guess that means you don't want to come to town tonight?" she says.

Jackie looks away, out the window.

But Ruby rolls her eyes and gets up, stomps out of the room. "I'm not going home with you," she snorts.

There is something sad in her voice.

She doesn't stay sad for long, though. After Jackie leaves, Ruby goes out every night, trying to avoid her mom's phone calls. She goes to the lake twice with some guy she meets at the roller rink and then, on the weekend, a sharp tap at the window wakes me well past midnight. I sit up in bed to find Ruby hissing at someone.

"Shut up!" Her finger at her mouth.

The guy outside sees me looking down from the top bunk and raises his open beer in salutation. Another figure stands behind him in the shadows, the red glare of a cigarette flaring and dying each time he brings it to his lips.

Ruby slides the window up. The cold night air sifts across my bare arms, drawing instant goosebumps.

"Wait a minute," she whispers.

"I'll be in the car." He lifts his chin to indicate where he's parked up the road, then waves to me and steps away from the window. I roll over and pull the covers up to my neck.

In the next minute I hear the sounds of a beer can being released by wet lips and the blowing of exhaled cigarette smoke. That other person clears his throat then, and without bothering to whisper, speaks thickly, a kind of hoarse grumble in the darkness.

"Why don't you come too?" His words crash through the darkness, flinging my eyes open again. "The lake's warm this time of night," he adds.

It's probably the most George has ever said to me.

I run into him on the street, parked outside the general store, the day after that first night together. I push through the whiny hinges of the screen door and recognize his shiny yellow convertible parked out front. He's turned around in his seat and I hesitate, but then he turns back and sees me. I wave tentatively, remembering other guys who hadn't wanted me to advertise that I knew them, and his face warms into a smile. But he doesn't call me over. Instead, he gets out of his car, leans against it and stares at me. I step down the stairs towards him and he crosses his arms while watching me, grinning.

"Hey," is all he says when I greet him. We stand before each other, behind sunglasses and groceries, and then he reaches for the bag and opens the door for me.

"Where are we going?" I ask.

George shrugs lazily, but he leans down and kisses my head—right on top like my dad does—and so I slide onto the front seat, all warm and fuzzy in his attention.

But George isn't much of a talker so it's still pretty quiet between us.

I'm comfortable out here at the edge of the lake, waves lapping beyond the meadow like a puppy at a bowl of milk and moonlight reflecting on the black shine. It's funny that I feel like I belong in this hokey place, but I suppose it's because I spent a lot of my childhood here. I don't miss the city like Dawne does, or crave its noisy brightness like Ruby. Back there I'd be smoking dope or dropping acid, giggling with boredom in the rich houses of my friends. And if someone like George drove by, slicked hair and turned-up collar, I'd be compelled to sneer at him, make some jibe about the weirdo greaseball. Now I'm wondering what, if George and I had more time—a whole fall and winter, maybe—this thing between us could turn into. Maybe it could take away the constant hunger I have.

So when he lets go of my hand and pulls me towards him, puts his hot, smokey tongue into my mouth and I can smell the rye or whatever was in that bottle, I'm too absorbed by his tongue to mind.

He starts to walk again, pulling me with him, tongues still bumping at each other. I open my eyes to peer sideways as we move, and then I look up at him. He is doing the same. I stop kissing him then, lean back in his arms and laugh loudly.

"Shhhh!" He covers my mouth with his hand, grinning. Next thing I know, I'm slung over his shoulder in a fireman's lift. He runs with me like that, legs on one side of his neck, head on the other, towards the water.

I feel like I'm going to puke again but before I can say anything, George slides me onto the sandy ground and gently lies on top of me. His head hovers beside mine and I can feel his excitement all over, the thudding pulse from the vein on his neck, his damp breath on my cheek. Then we roll and tumble against each other, hot tongues and hot breath in the summer night and the urgency is unfamiliar, dizzying. When George rolls off some moments later, I am disappointed, but relieved. We lie in the sandy grass, listen to each other gasp for air, fish out of water.

Dawne is what people at school call *experienced*. She tells me that the sweaty pawing with some boy at the end of a night is what it's all about and that she's no different from most girls, only more honest. Me, I've always tried to avoid those awkward moments of darkness after a date, the preliminaries before the "Good night." But guys always end up driving me home in knife-cutting silence, as if they can't wait to end the nightmare. Or they bring me flowers the next time, as if that'll get them past my jeans. It's different with George, though. He just sits there, tickles me with his eyes, making me want to stay here. It's as if I never really left the lake at all; as if I was meant to grow up here beside him.

I remember one of the first times I picked raspberries. I must have been three or four, wandering up and down the rows, helping myself to the fat, red berries at eye level, stuffing them in my mouth instead of the tiny plastic bucket I held. And I remember Cal's voice calling me from somewhere beyond the wall of green canes, his face when he found me and then his huge laugh at the stains all over my face, my hands, my sundress. I remember how he caught me in his two arms, swung me over his shoulder and carried me off to the others. How he rubbed my back after I puked on the berries later.

I'd like to move beyond the barriers between George and me, but I don't know how. I don't know much about sex; don't know if I'm ready for it. And George never talks, so how do I know what's going on for him, either?

But when I'm back in my bunk remembering how it felt to be pushed so close together, lifting and pressing like some kind of fairground ride, then I start to think about going all the way. I get excited, imagining what it could lead to.

Once I complained to Dawne about guys and their one-track minds and she laughed at me.

"Some girls want it too," was what she said.

I'm wondering if that's what I'm feeling with George.

He's half-sitting up now, tugging at my T-shirt, trying to take it off. Even though I freeze up inside when I think about him staring at me undressed, I don't stop him. I'm caught up in the idea that it's me he wants right now. So I help him, half-rolling on one side and then the other, pulling the shirt over my head when it catches on my ears.

But when his hard-on pushes against me, I'm scared. It's not the same kind of scared as when the police brought me home one night at 3:00 a.m., rang the doorbell and handed me over to my dad. This is the kind of scared that happens when you know you have a choice to make; a choice that might affect the rest of your life. It makes me dizzy to think about it.

So when George puts his warm palm over my breast, I am both relieved and petrified. And then I think the smile on my face must mean I'm in love. But when he puts his hand between my legs, holding it there so I can feel the heat through my jeans, I blank out. I know I'm supposed to like it, but what I'm feeling is minor panic. I hold my eyes shut tight, in case he's looking at me for a reaction, and I kind of pray to myself. I'm not religious, but this feeling I get when he does that—a kind of explosion down low inside—is nothing I've felt before. Maybe it's God talking to me, I don't know.

I hear the metallic click of my jeans' zipper as George pulls the tab and then slips his hand inside. He covers my belly with his rough palm, massages me down low. There's a flooding warmth moving through me and I want to arch my back and push against his hand, but I hold on to the feeling of fear that lingers behind the other feeling, the one that wants to devour him.

I think what's missing is George's voice, some pretty words, maybe. Maybe if he spoke he could persuade me.

I've started dreaming about George a lot.

"Are you sure it isn't Adonis?" Ruby laughs at me.

Dawne smirks. "That just means you're horny, girl."

Maybe they're right. Maybe the man in my dreams is someone I'd like George to be. Because the George in the shadows of my sleep—the dream George—actually talks. He picks me up after work and we joke all the way to a skinny-dipping beach on the other side of the lake. Over a fire in the dark, our mouths form silent words, silent laughter, silent happiness. Later we dance on the pier at the end of the lake, swinging round and round like an old couple on the Lawrence Welk show. Another night we climb over the fence of the roller rink after it's closed, skate together singing "Blueberry Hill" and "Ebony Eyes," songs they play over the hi-fi speakers during the day.

But the closest George and me have ever come to a real conversation is the time we bought a pint of strawberry ice cream and drove up behind the army camp to eat it. We had to use our fingers because we forgot the wooden spoons in the store's freezer, but we had fun feeding each other and staring through the chain-link fence at the soldiers.

"Maybe I'll join the military," he said, wiping a strawberry smear off his chin with the back of his hand.

It came out of nowhere and I was so surprised that I laughed, a kind of honking burst. I couldn't picture George with a crewcut, so I figured he was joking, but when I looked at him I saw he was thinking out loud and that shut me up fast.

He nodded to himself, oblivious to me. "Free education. Good pay. A future."

I take his wrist where it sticks out of my underpants and pull his searching fingers away from their goal.

He buries his face against my neck, shuddering as he rocks against me, and I can smell the oil in his hair as it rubs against my cheek.

"I know," he says.

But I don't think he does.

He gets up and I lean on my elbow as he moves toward the nearby shadows. I hear the sound of his pee as he aims into the bushes and I think of Dawne back in the car, moaning and rubbing against Whatsisname as if she was in the middle of a bad nightmare. I'm wondering if I should just go up to George, put my hands on his shoulders and tell him I want to do it but don't know how.

Instead I lie back down and close my eyes. I think about what it means to be a couple, standing together side by side for a picture, a fat baby holding our hands and a yellow kitchen behind us and that warm, home feeling. So when George's tongue touches my nipple again, the huge groan that comes from my mouth surprises me in mid-breath. A powerful shiver spreads up my thighs and I feel like some kind of Amazon woman, wanting to squeeze this man against me. But then he takes away the heat of his mouth and the chill on my wet skin makes me feel suddenly disconnected, empty. My nipples turn to raisins in the cold night air.

I'm glad George can't see me in the raspberry fields. I look like some peasant, a bandana around my neck and a straw hat on my head, long-sleeved shirt and jeans to protect me from the thorns and snakes. I shuffle along, sweat trickling down my scratched hands and a hump on my shoulders like an old Doukhobor woman. My thoughts wander under the broiling sun and I think about living the rest of my life in sleepy little Yarrow with George. I wonder if we'd get married in a church and whether he's from a religious family and then I wonder if he'd talk more if I were a good Lutheran girl.

I wish I knew whether George even thinks about what's going on between us.

He rolls off me onto his back, picks up my T-shirt and lays it on top of my chest. I keep my eyes closed, hoping he'll talk, snuggle up to me and whisper "Please?" then use his darting tongue on my ear or say pretty words like the men in those dumb nurse books. I open my eyes when I smell sulphur and hear a match flame, watch him light his cigarette and sigh the smoke out of his nose. We lie like that for a long time, staring up at the stars. I find the Big Dipper, Orion's belt, Pegasus and

Cassiopeia before I get tired of waiting, then I roll onto my side and put my hand inside his shirt. I like the coarseness of the hair on his chest, the bristly feel beneath my palm as I rub my hand over his heart.

"It's late," I announce in case he hasn't noticed. His head nods slowly up and down as the smoke streams out of his nostrils.

I watch the red ember of his flicked cigarette as it arcs beneath the dark sky, see it land and die out. George puts his hand on top of mine, still on his chest.

"Time for a swim." He says this as though we've always swum together, with a history of summer nights at the lake. I let myself be swallowed up by the rarity of those words. I consider that, in George's mind, we may already be a couple and I am touched.

He runs ahead of me, pulling his shirt off as he goes and turning to fling it at me. The shirt whips at my cheek and I grab for it as it slips away. I hold it to my face, breathe in its smell—cigarettes, rye and something unnameably male—and I take that scent deep inside me.

And when I join him in the lake, I feel the lapping waves of water against my skin like the flicks of his tongue and I want to stay here always.

So I say it.

"I want to stay here with you, George." I try to sound like the sultry women of those old black and white movies, but my voice comes out like a scared little girl's. The sound carries over the water like a whining dog.

And what does he do? He laughs at me, like my brother did, as if I'm being funny. Then he slaps his arm against the surface of the lake, sending a wave of water into my face. The water hits me before I see it coming, catches me with eyes and mouth wide open. And maybe that's a good thing, because it carries away the hot rush of tears on the brim of my eyelids, washing them into the lake.

My brother Cal died when I was thirteen. I never had a chance to ask him about those shadowy meetings below the stairs at Sunnyside Market. I never got to talk to him about what it's like to be the other half, the guy in my situation. I'm glad he had the experience of love or whatever it is, but I feel cheated that I didn't get to ask him all the questions I have now.

When the raspberry season ends, nothing has changed between George and me. On our last night together, he gives me a big hug goodbye but he never asks how to find me, only talks some more about joining the army. I get out of his car for the last time and close the passenger door softly, a large stone in my throat.

The next day the bus pulls out of the local Greyhound station and I twist my head to look out the window, telling myself to memorize everything about this place in case I ever get back here again. But it's not likely I will return, or not to this place, anyway. So I guess what I'm really doing is searching for a yellow Chevy convertible, hoping it will appear before the bus merges onto the highway, cutting off the driver and forcing him to stop.

Beyond the window the neat squares of fields and acres of black and white cows beside sparse farmhouses seem foreign and strange. The bus roars onto the highway and I sit with my restlessness, unable to understand why the summer feels so unfinished.

Home Free

I am remembering how my mother explained a *faux pas* to me. Sitting at the kitchen table, doing French homework, a translation of Molière, Balzac, somebody—I can't now remember the author or the content of the piece. I only remember reading the lines out to my educated mother, a woman with French, German and Latin schooling.

I came to the unfamiliar phrase and pronounced it the way it looked like it should sound.

"It was the worst ... fox paw? ... of the century."

What I remember is the ringing sound of Mother's laughter where she stood at the deep enamel sink, arms in bubbles up to her elbows, washing loaf pans, mixing bowls, measuring spoons. Baking day, the whole kitchen drenched in the sweet smell of comfort.

And my mother, coming over to me with soapsuds still on her arms, wrapping their warm wetness around my neck and the bubbles popping in my nose.

"Fox paw! Oh, that's lovely, Julie!" As if I'd said something too fine to forget, the way kids sometimes do, the way Stephanie does now.

I'm sitting at that same table when my father comes home today. It's a chrome-legged table with a grey, swirling, Formica top. He's looking all of his almost seventy years.

He gives me a funny kind of smile and sits down, puts his stubby fingers together on top of the table. He sits there as if he's considering what to say, looking out the window at the branches of a big maple lifting and falling in the breeze.

When he finally speaks, he says only one thing: "He's dying."

The words make a sound in my brain like marbles clattering up one side of a china bowl and down the other. I want to get up and walk out of the room but I don't. Instead I nod dumbly.

Because it's my Uncle Gus he's talking about and there's not much I want to say about him.

Later I go visit Auntie Marge, who looks like she hasn't slept at all since the night of Gus's stroke. She stands at the door, not registering who I am until my cousin appears behind her.

"Oh, Julie—it's so awful!" Cindy flings herself at me and over her shoulder I see how Auntie Marge stands frozen, a weak smile on her face.

When Cindy lets go, I encircle my aunt's wide girth, feeling her heaviness like some huge rock in my arms. If I could, I would transfer the burden to my own shoulders. But I am only the niece.

Cindy complains about how worn out she is with all the driving back and forth to the hospital and then having to go home to make meals for her own children as well as a husband who doesn't care, doesn't help, only wants to know what's for dinner. Marge sits complacently while Cindy lists her woes.

"I'll take her," I say as Cindy pours me some tea. Her eyes lift to stare incredulously and the tea slops over the brim of the cup.

Marge puts her large, warm hand over mine and Cindy scuttles back to the kitchen for a dishcloth.

I lay my other hand on top of Marge's and squeeze. "I'm happy to drive you to the hospital, Auntie Marge."

Her eyes water but the tight lines around their edges relax slightly.

Cindy mops the spilled tea and gushes, "That's great, Julie!"

Uncle Gus half sits, half lies in his hospital bed, eyes shut and hair splayed across the pillow. At seventy-six his hair is still thick with rich waves, but it is no longer the fiery beacon that convinced Marge he was some kind of red-haired Prince Charming. She sits beside him, rests her palm on his head to stroke his hair.

His eyes open halfway and one side of his mouth lifts into a trembling smile. His good hand, the one that still works, rises off the bed with an effort and Marge reaches for it. As she does, I see the sunlight from the window playing across the red sheen on his arms. The hair that covers his body.

"Look who I brought to visit today, Gus." Marge pats the chair beside her. "Come sit down, Julie."

She doesn't notice that I remain standing. She concentrates on wiping the drool from Gus's chin.

"How was lunch, dear?" The tissue jabs at a wet spot on Gus's shoulder. "You had your medicine?" The hands straighten his nightgown. "Doctor been in?"

I wait, a long, arduous moment, as Gus's mouth struggles to make a sensible sound. I want to clamp my palm against his slobbering lips and then I want to yell at my aunt for believing Gus can answer her.

Instead I excuse myself to escape down the hall to the gift store. I look at the shelves of stuffed animals, the racks of bestsellers and the other goods they sell to lift the spirits of the sick—manicure kits, earring trees, brush and comb sets—things to help the visitors feel loving, caring, helpful.

At the cash register there is a pyramid of camera film behind a framed photo: two grandparents, two parents, two children, one of each sex. But no uncles and aunts, I think. No cousins. I pay for my candy and magazine, then go to the lobby.

I wait half an hour, eating chocolate and reading Hollywood gossip. Returning to the room, I find Marge busy smoothing the sheets under Gus's lumpy body. When she folds back the covers to make a nurse's corner, a slender calf, white skin covered in scant red hair, is revealed. The fragility makes me swallow.

"Auntie Marge—" I say in a soft voice, and when she turns, startled, I point at my watch. "I have a class in an hour."

She stares at me blankly before comprehending. Then she leans over Gus to plant a red kiss on his cheek and I see his brown eyes staring at me from beside her cloud of grey hair. I stare back, unsure whether the stroke has affected his sight.

"You be good," Marge says, lifting her husband's hand. She lets go and the hand drops to the bed with a soft thud.

Her eyes fill as she turns and I put my hand on her shoulder. Marge takes my arm and I am surprised by the strength of her grip.

"I'll end up in hospital like Daddy if I have to take care of Mother by myself," Cindy whines to her sister.

Louise—the one who didn't inherit Gus's red hair—comes into town to stay with her mother.

I phone Louise and offer my help.

"Maybe if you took Gus Jr. for a while?" she says. "Then Mom and I can visit Daddy longer."

They deliver three-year-old Gus and when he arrives, Stephanie, at five, insists she can't play with a boy, even a cousin. But she allows Gus to watch her for a few minutes, then changes her mind and recruits him for the part of Maid Marion in her rendition of Robin Hood. An hour and a half later, annoyed by his enslavement, Gussy announces he wants to go home and Stephanie hits him for not finishing the game. When Louise phones, I tell her that today needs to be a short day and, with Gus Jr. in tears, we return to Marge's.

Louise receives her snuffling son with loud kisses. "Oh, sweetie!" she says, gathering him into a hug. "Don't cry—I love you and so does

Gamma and Big Gussy. And I bet Stephie wants to give you a kiss better, don't you, Steph?"

Stephanie makes a face. Louise looks from her to me as if to say, "Aren't you going to do something about her?"

I put my hands on Stephie's shoulders and steer her back to the car while she tries to shrug me off. I am buckling her into the seat as Louise approaches, Gus still in her arms.

"Try again tomorrow?" I say apologetically.

Louise puts Gus down and looks a question at him. From where he is buried in her thigh, the boy shakes his head.

"I'll call you later," Louise says. She leans to plant a wet blur of lipstick on my cheek and I try not to wince. Then she pokes her head into the back seat of the car and blows a kiss at Stephanie. Stephanie returns the kiss by making sloppy sucking noises on her hand.

"Bye, Red." Louise waves at her.

My hand on the driver's door, I look back at Stephanie. "It's not really red," I say, frowning at my daughter's curls. "More strawberry blonde."

Louise laughs. "That's the colour of Cindy's hair when she was little. She's going to be as loud a redhead as Aunty Cindy, isn't she, Gussy?"

Pulled against his mother's side, Gus Jr.'s face is distorted by the squeeze of Louise's palm and thigh. He tries to nod but only succeeds in making himself look abnormal.

It's what I think about as I drive away from my aunt's house, whether my family is abnormal.

At the first stop sign, Stephanie interrupts my thoughts. "When I'm grown up, I'm going to look just like Aunty Cindy!"

"Maybe," I remind her. "We have to wait and see."

"I'm sorry you don't have pretty hair like mine, Mommy."

In the rear-view mirror she looks sad as she shakes her head, those red-hued curls bouncing around her face. She sees me looking and blows another loud kiss.

"That's to make you feel better," she croons.

"You're such a sweetie," I tell her. But I'm wondering whether she's too young to have her hair dyed.

Dad sprawls in the La-z-Boy, an open photo album on his lap. His hands hang from the armrests, a beer can in one. I tiptoe in case he's dozing, but his eyes lift at my approach.

He gives me a tired smile and I sit on the arm of the couch.

"Do you remember this?" His finger indicates a picture and I crane my head to look. An old black and white shot, one of many family scenes that change to colour later on in the album. There is Granny Harris in dark dress and lace collar, birdlike hands clasped at her stomach. Granddad in pin-striped suit with vest, arm around Granny's waist. Mom in a full-skirted dress and Dad in a jungle-print shirt over Bermudas. Cindy and Louise in their perpetual crinolines and necklaces and frilly ankle socks. Uncle Gus, with oiled hair combed straight back, the redness vivid in spite of the black and white film, short-sleeved shirt open at the neck to reveal a hairy chest. Marge beside him, plump and garish in an outsized muumuu. And at the very edge of the photo, as if I'm trying to escape, a younger me in pedal pushers and striped sailor shirt, sweat-dampened hair and heat-flushed cheeks.

The photo must have interrupted one of the endless hide and seek games played at my cousins' house, games I always won because of a secret hiding place. Near the back porch, behind the unpruned juniper with its terrible rashy itch, through a curtain of droopy willow branches and into the shadows of a little close beneath, I watched the others comb the yard for me. With a perfect view of the back door, that place designated as Home, I'd crouch for what seemed like hours, staring at the north arm of the Fraser River and the clouds of smoke from woodchip burners along its south bank. I'd search the distant mountains for the place where my father said the United States began and I'd get lost in my head while waiting to be found. When I heard footsteps, I'd hold my breath and wait for the seeker to pass before I made my move, scrunching backwards through the bushes and up the porch stairs, touching the door handle and yelling, "Home free!"

But if Uncle Gus stepped out that back door while I was hiding, I'd shrink down, try to squeeze into the ground or the prickle of junipers. And I'd regret my red shorts or yellow T-shirt, colours that screamed like neon from the midst of all that greenery.

Seeing him there, squinting as he drew on his cigarette and staring around the garden, I'd curl into the ground like a sleeping dog. The hand with the cigarette periodically lifted to stroke the red moustache, a preening thumb and forefinger on each side of his open mouth. In the wavering light of late-afternoon sun, the body hair on the chest, arms and legs of my uncle glowed like a strange red aura beneath that glistening halo of oiled hair.

"I remember some things," I tell my father.

I look at the photo again to see where Gus stands in relation to me. His arm stretches behind Marge's neck but it's my shoulders that hunch protectively.

Dad closes the photo album and takes a last slug of beer.

"Guess there's no point going back there," he says.

Louise tells me that Marge wants to visit Gus more often. If I could take her to the hospital in the afternoons, Louise suggests, she or Cindy could take her mornings and evenings.

"If Stephie came here, that would be better," Louise says, then rushes to add, "for Gussy, I mean."

I know in every family there is one who fails the test. But I'm not sure why Louise thinks it's me.

Dad is at the hospital on his lunch break when Marge and I arrive. He sits close to the door, away from his brother, as though what's happened to Gus might be contagious. But Gus, reduced to the functions of three clear tubes running in and out of his stomach, his veins, his bladder, can never be a threat again.

Marge lays her hand on Gus's forearm to let him know she is there, but he does not respond. His eyes remain shut and his fingers curl tightly into his palm; where his hand should be there is only a fuzz of red-haired knuckles, like a paw.

On each black page of the family photo albums, Uncle Gus's hands curve round a woman's shoulder, his fingers cupping her like a snug-fitting toque at the top of her sleeve. First it is Marge and his mother, then Marge and my mother, and eventually each of his daughters are caught in a paw. I am not far into the album before one of my own shoulders is clutched and Gus's furry arm tickles the back of my neck. I step sideways to squeeze against one model-perfect cousin or the other and the grip of those hairy knuckles tightens. In the photos I am caught forever between Gus and Cindy or Gus and Louise, their winning smiles emphasizing my dark scowl, the unnatural tightness of my jaw.

As a kid I have no choice: whenever my dad visits his brother, I'm taken along too.

"Hi, honey!" Marge's fleshy arms reach out, pull me into her over-perfumed bosom. "How ya doing?"

I endure the suffocating hug, listening to the muffle of Marge's voice from between the two mounds of breast, and then her palms squeeze my cheeks and my face is tilted up towards her powdered nose and outsized red lips.

In the midst of her gushing, I see Gus waiting. He catches my eye and his face crinkles into a leer that is supposed to be a smile, irises swallowed by wrinkles, and I am left with nothing but his red crown for a landmark.

And when Marge releases me, Gus sidles forward, turning sideways like a boxer and shooting a pretend jab at my ribs or stomach. When I step away, he leans suddenly into my face, everything distorted by his closeness and presumption.

"How's my Julie, eh?" His moustache against my ear, his mouth so close that the scent of cigarettes and hair oil nauseates. My eyes search frantically for my mother and aunt and I whimper as I see them disappear into the kitchen.

"You got a little kiss for your uncle?"

I don't want to, can't, and my lips pinch together until they are as immoveable as the Say-No-Evil monkey on my bureau. But Gus doesn't accept refusals. The only way out is to let everything inside turn black with cold.

I can still feel the rise in my throat.

Years later, trying for adult empathy, I complain to my parents. It is, apparently, the worst kind of faux pas.

"He gives me the creeps," I whine.

My mother rolls her eyes. "For heaven's sake, Julie."

She leaves me at the sink, cleaning up after another family gathering. From the living room, collecting dirty dishes, she calls back, "He's your uncle."

Dad enters with empty beer bottles jammed on the ends of his fingers. His eyebrows lift at my scowl.

"She says she doesn't like Gus," Mom answers Dad's unasked question.

He turns away with an angry frown. Standing above the cardboard beer case, he drops the empties one by one so that each knocks against the glass of another with a dangerous clink.

Mom thumps more dirty dishes beside me. Both of them avoid my eyes.

"He makes me kiss him," I blurt.

"And we make you do chores," says Mom. She turns to let Dad untie her apron.

When he finally looks up, there is pain in his eyes, as though he needs my understanding. "Gus is family, Julie."

When my mother died, I moved home to help my father. There were regular dinner invitations from Marge, which I as regularly declined, pleading Stephanie's bedtime. But one day I came home to find Stephanie on the phone, Dad watching from the kitchen table with a grin on his face.

"... and then we went to the gosery store and we gotted some macaronis for dinner ..." Stephanie listed off the items from their afternoon shopping trip and I smiled too.

"Who is it?" I whispered to Dad.

"Marge."

"Okay," Stephanie said. "I'll ask." She turned to us with a big smile: "Auntie Marj'rie wants to know if we can come for Gus's birthday party." Then she hesitated, adding a throaty whisper: "But do I like roast beast, Mommy?"

Dad laughed as he took the receiver from Stephie. I wasn't sure it was funny.

The welcome ritual was the same.

"I can't breathe, Auntie Marj'rie!" Stephanie squealed when Marge hugged her.

I hovered as Gus approached and Cindy and Louise urged their kids to "Give Grandpa a kiss." Darlene, Cindy's youngest, wrestled frantically as Gus lifted her and aimed his lips, pouted and wrinkled and menacing. She turned her face in terror and when the kiss landed on her cheek, she howled.

"Oh no!" Cindy groaned. "It's another Julie!"

The others tittered, amused.

Gus Jr. brushed his grandfather aside like so much dust and Gus turned to Stephanie.

He stooped in front of her with his wrinkled face, pointed a hairy finger at his cheek. Stephanie stared in wonder until Gus reached for her wrists with determination. Without waiting, I swooped, swinging Stephanie beyond his reach.

"You can just ask her, Uncle Gus. Do you want to give your Great-uncle Gus a kiss, Stephie?" I felt the hugeness of Stephanie's eyes as I turned back to Gus. "I'd rather you let her choose."

His bushy eyebrows lifted in surprise and then he shrugged and turned away. I heard his growled derision as the kitchen door swung shut behind him. "What the hell's with that girl?"

Cradling the back of her head with the palm of my hand, I buried Stephanie's face in my neck. "Did he scare you?" I whispered.

In the kitchen Gus continued. "All I did was give her a kiss. Or try to."

And Marge's answer: "Why can't you leave things be instead of always stirring them up?"

Stephanie arched to get out of my arms. She leaped away from me, calling, "Unca Gus?"

After dinner Gus announced another family photo shoot. The kids were playing when he called them to the veranda.

"Just a minute, Unca Gus," Stephanie told him. "I'm Joan of Arc and I'm being burned right now." She stretched her arms at the imaginary stake and the younger children fed the magnificent fire beneath her.

Gus chortled as he turned to Dad. "Harris," he gestured. "Get your drunken ass over here and take a picture of me and my bride! C'mere, Margie."

Seated in his folding aluminum chair, Gus patted his skinny lap as if inviting a dog. And Marge pshawed, pleased, as she swayed across the hot deck toward her man, lowering her broad beam as delicately as possible. Gus crossed his eyes as she landed on him, turning his face for everyone to see.

"Oof!" he complained, putting down his glass of Johnny Walker, then sliding his hand up Marge's leg, opening his eyes wide and staring around the veranda.

"Mind yourself in front of the children, Gus Harris!" Marge shoved at his hand.

He chuckled, gave her a slap on the thigh and Dad snapped the shot. When Marge got up, Gus looked at me and winked. "How 'bout my other girlfriend?" he asked. "Let's have a picture of me and Julie."

Gus got up and moved toward me, standing behind my chair. He bent, folding his arms across my chest and resting his chin on my shoulder.

"I never got a kiss hello from you, sweetie," Gus said.

A sharp hush fell over the veranda. I held my breath and closed my eyes and pecked at the area near Gus's mouth. He pressed his prickly face against my cheek and then his wet, bristly lips.

Kicking and thrashing, I clawed my way out of the chair and made for the house. Behind me I heard Stephanie calling, "Mommy, we need you for the family pitcher!"

Stephanie asks, "Can I go see Uncle Gus?"

I'm not sure about young children and death, but apparently Marge is.

"He'd love to see you, honey! Make his day."

"He might scare you," I tell Stephanie when Marge goes for her coat. "He doesn't look very nice."

Stephanie shakes her curls at me, unconcerned.

I push on the heavy door and Stephanie squeezes past me to look at Gus. She climbs onto his bed and tips her red head against one of his sunken cheeks, puts a small hand on the other side of his face. Gus's eyes lift to look at Marge, and I wonder if what I see there is emotion.

His lip trembles as he makes an indiscernible sound. Marge moves forward, tilts her ear toward him. "What's that, dear?"

Gus mumbles again and Marge leans closer. But after a moment she straightens up, head shaking in confusion and face tight with alarm.

"I don't know what he wants," she chokes and her eyes pinch shut. I put my arms around her and hold tight as the shaking begins.

"It's okay, Auntie Marj'rie," says Stephanie. "I can help."

I stop rubbing Marge's back and watch Stephanie's red hair falling across Gus's face. For a long second there is nothing but the wet sound of a noisy kiss echoing through the room.

"See?" Stephanie sits back. "He's smiling now!"

Gus's face is quiet, his eyes and mouth drooling.

I am holding my breath as I step backwards, hand reaching behind me. When my extended fingers contact the cold steel of the door handle, I turn and push hard.

But as I clear the threshold, I see two curled red paws on the bed-sheets, waiting to die.

Homing Instinct

A rtie's shoe pushes at a tear in the carpet as he talks. I watch the way his toe nudges at the rose-beige broadloom, an ugly sculpted job from the 1950s.

"I got a letter from that art school in California," he's explaining. "They liked my portfolio." When he looks up, I feel his eyes wrap around me like so much west coast fog. "I figure I've got enough saved up now." He shrugs. And I nod, unsure of what he's trying to say.

My mother brushes past—"The Johnstones are here, dear. Can you get George a drink?"—and the opportunity to escape leaps at me. I turn to go, glancing apologetically at Artie but he's already back at that well-worked hole in the floor.

Right now it seems like everything I touch ends up dead. It makes me wonder if—how much—I should try to keep this relationship alive. Artie's been around for some tough years but nothing seems to prevent the Big D from taking what it wants in my life.

And besides, Artie's timing stinks. We're at my sister's wake, for God's sake, and here he's wanting to talk about leaving. I sigh as I drop two ice cubes into a tumbler of Scotch, then head towards the front door where Mr. Johnstone, the neighbour, stands with his hand on my father's shoulder.

I know Artie's had enough. We've all had enough. Four and a half years with Sheila's leukemia has taken its toll.

Mr. Johnstone takes the glass from my hand and leans to give me a hug. Across the room I see Artie staring in a hypnotic trance and somewhere inside I feel myself slipping. I don't know, as Mr. Johnstone voices his condolences, if it's the welling memory of Sheila or the sudden gape of future ahead of me that causes a rush of renewed tears. I thank Mr. Johnstone and head back to Artie, wanting only to get lost in all that fog, not be left alone in this cold, northern place.

He is back to worrying the worn bit of carpet as I approach. I touch his elbow and when he looks up, brow lifted in the form of a question, I don't wait. Without thinking about it, without even considering how it will affect the rest of my life, I say, "Can I come with you?"

Artie's smile belongs in one of those expensive magazine ads, the ones where a macho-but-tender man snuggles with a woman in front of a fire or under an umbrella. When he smiles at me now, I have this feeling I've said the right thing. For an instant I'm blinded by the prettiness of the scene we create, the golden light of that magazine picture all around us. But when he leans his temple against mine and pulls me into him, my spine shrinks a little, as if a string were tightening along the gather of bones, and the vertebrae at the back of my neck crack with the force of his hug.

When we first see Sacramento, I shudder at the frosting of smog above strip lights that seem to stretch for miles. We drive by car lots and fast-food outlets, the bane of American existence, and I wonder how far beyond my window is the California fantasized by northerners like us.

We rent a house and spend the first two days lying on the cool tiles of the living room floor, amazed at the sound of kids romping outside in 115-degree heat. We leave the air conditioner off, afraid of utility costs in a land where rivers are sparse and hydroelectricity is sometimes imported from Canada. We tell each other that eventually we'll acclimatize, here in the land of the free where nothing is free.

And then, on the third evening, we venture out. In the still-simmering dusk we move nervously, like neighbourhood cats padding through tangled gardens and backyard jungles, ogling camellias the size of giant rhododendrons and palms leaping from the earth like towering umbrellas. At the first shrill of cicadas, our hands reach reflexively for each other's and when the cool desert air sweeps in from the east, we run down the middle of the street, fingers entwined like a passion flower vine, laughing at our delicate state.

"We're icebergs in Hell!" I yell from the top of a rise when we stop to admire the panorama of rolling hills and yellow grasslands running away north, home.

In those first weeks, it is Artie who seems disgruntled by the reality of this new home. After riding his bike in the carbon monoxide-laden environment, he bursts through the door with a loud complaint. "I don't know how anyone can live here!" He rants about the American automobile fetish while I take a bottle of water from the fridge to cool his fever. He gulps at its coldness, then reaches for more.

"It's like breathing smoke from a campfire!" Water slops across the counter as he overpours the glass. I reach around him to rescue my sketch pad and carry it to the table.

I'm still in nursing mode from those last days with Sheila so my voice brightens in reaction to his mood. "Want to see my new drawings?" I ask.

He turns around, brow lifted in a question, and then sees the gallery of strange plants spread across the table. I show him my "asparagus" tree, "sword" and "spear" cacti, names I've given my discoveries like an explorer of uncharted territory, and he smiles that smile again. But when the neighbour's car revs outside, his face darkens and he returns to more lamentations about California roads, California weather, Californians. I look out the window at the yellowness of the land beyond, dehydrated and wrinkled like those dancing television raisins, and feel a stirring within.

Someone once told me that the ends of things—life stages, relation-ships—announce themselves in dreams. During those early Sacramento months, my dreams are full of Sheila, the sister who'd wanted to be a dancer. I dream about the hours spent in her hospital room, talking to fill its emptiness while she lay there, so drugged she couldn't talk, couldn't eat, couldn't puke, probably couldn't hear me. I dream about holding her fish-cold hand while babbling about the future, the kids and the family dinners we were going to have.

One night, Sheila tugs her hand out of mine, pulls tubes of dull-coloured liquids from her body and pushes her feet over the side of the white bed, standing tentatively on the two twig-thin legs beneath her gown. She takes a step forward and I watch as her failing body turns light and feathery, rising up like gossamer in the wind and dancing, dancing on her toes. She dances over and around and through me, transparent except for her two dark eyes like beads of jet. When she dances near the window, she stops and looks outside. I try to persuade her back to bed then, but she only flashes those black eyes at me and climbs onto the windowsill, launches herself into space.

In late November the temperatures drop and Artie stops talking about going north for Christmas, "to a civilized climate." We drive to Lake Tahoe one weekend, passing through green farmland and old mining towns, and I buy Christmas cards with scenes of the ski resort in win-ter. I sign the insides of the cards from both of us, though Artie shakes his head at them. "That's probably man-made snow." His finger jabs at the picture. "They don't have real snow here."

"He's happiest at school," I write home to Canada. "He's made some good friends. We grow well again." I ignore the hopeful comment in his parents' last letter about the prospect of future grandchildren.

We tried to have a baby once. It was right after we found out Sheila had leukeumia and then I had to walk around with this big secret inside of me so that everyone could focus on my sister. When I finally told Sheila about the baby, because I had to fill up the emptiness in that room somehow, her eyes bulged like fishbowls. I think I was more scared than she was then: scared of what lay ahead of us; scared that she might leave me to be a mother by myself.

"Have you chosen any names yet?" she asked from the white depths of pillows. And when I looked at her lying there, so weak and transparent, I had to keep her going somehow.

"Artie likes 'Sheila' for a girl," I smiled. "But then there'd be two of you answering whenever we call, so maybe not, eh?"

Sheila's head shook slowly. "Don't," she said before closing her eyes.

Afterwards, after she'd slid into a permanent silence and I couldn't tell if she was sleeping or slipping across the line, I wondered if she'd given up, let the cancer cells wrap her up and carry her off.

But the baby died before Sheila. Didn't even make it through the first trimester. The doctor called Artie and me into his office so we knew something was wrong, but when he pulled out the ultrasound picture, Artie turned away from its tiny blur.

"We'll have to schedule you for a D&C, Shawn." The doctor's concerned glance fell on Artie, then me. "The baby's been dead for some time."

Two wet trickles struggled past the stubble on Artie's cheek and he raised his hand to cover his brow. I reached to lay my hand on his arm, but he couldn't look at me. We sat in the doctor's office, our two chairs and our grief side by side, separated by the space between us. Later, alone in a hospital room below Sheila's, I curled up like a foetus and sobbed. Long shudders ran over and through me like a dying heartbeat, but in the middle of that heaving night, there was more than a life lost between us.

By the time Sacramento's strip malls are hung with Christmas lights, I'm immune to the bizarre Californian practice of juxtaposing other

realities against the desert. Walking by muffled Edwardian carol-
lers huddled beneath a date palm, I barely notice the incongruity,
drawn instead by the hills beyond. There is something out there that
beckons—urges—me.

My dreams move outside the whiteness of a hospital room and into
the lush northwest panorama of my childhood. Sheila and I tumble
and roll beneath the waving boughs of giant firs and cedars and when
I wake from those restless sleeps, the drylands beyond my window are
a shock. But when, in the mystical light of a desert dawn, the backyard
roosters and urban goats raise their chant to the bleat of traffic, my
disorientation recedes with the dreams.

As the Christmas holidays approach, Artie starts thinking about the
north and home again. Soon the inevitable occurs.

He stands over our thrift-store toaster one morning, babysitting its
burning ritual and trying to be casual when he speaks: "Why don't we
try getting pregnant again, Shawn?"

A cold draught sifts across the back of my neck, icy fingers lingering
against my skin. I have to look outside, find the shadows of sun and
trees to know I'm still here, south of winter.

"Maybe." My shoulders lift in an involuntary shiver. "Maybe we
should wait 'til we have medical insurance again."

"But that's the thing." He heads for the table with his plate of toast,
perfectly browned and exactly buttered. "The baby wouldn't be born
until we get home. We'll just start it here." He puts a hand on my
shoulder, bends down to kiss me, eyes wide open.

I know this is an important moment, but it's like I'm moving through
him as I wander into the fog of those eyes. When he starts talking
again, his voice low and whispery in my consciousness, I'm climbing
those dry, rolling hills behind the city, hearing the constant hum of
birdsong that haunts the valley by daylight, belying the picture of death
in those parched hills.

I bend my neck to admire the bigness of the California sky and feel its invitation. Up here, so close to Sheila's home, I wonder about my sister and my baby, high above me somewhere, and I close my eyes to imagine what they'd look like now. And then, from some dark cupboard of memory, the strangest vision escapes. I feel the softness of a summer lawn beneath my feet, the hot damp of my skin as I chase after baby Sheila. In front of me, bowlegged by the bulk of diapers and unbalanced by a worried look back over her shoulder, she teeters before sitting down hard, prevented from escape.

"What is it, Sheila? What have you got?" She stretches her clenched fist away and my big sister hands pry at the closed fingers.

"No!"

"Sheila, show Shawn."

"No!" she twists from me as I wrap my arms around her from behind.

And when I unpeel those baby-sized fingers, inside the pinkness is a butterfly, half dead from compression. Its oversized eyes, two beads of jet, stare accusingly.

Artie pats my shoulder as he straightens up again. "Not ready yet, huh?" He moves around the other side of the table, sits across from me, but I see his look is wrong. "It's not going to happen again, you know, Shawn."

And I'm not sure if he's talking about babies or death.

A week later, Artie brings home a gift for our unconceived child— "Something I made in my spare time." He shrugs, wraps it in special baby-shower paper and puts it under the spindly Christmas tree beside the other gifts that wait there.

Now every time I walk by the living room, that lumpy package of yellow and blue and pink accuses me, pricking me with the memories of hospitals and funerals and death. For some reason that gift seems more out of place than the sprayed-on snowdrifts and plastic holly of this Sacramento Christmas.

Artie's face clouds over when my next period arrives. For a while he is quiet with his mood, but then he breaks into a fury, blaming me, blaming himself, blaming fate. When I try to talk to him about it, he tells me he can't, doesn't want to, won't.

"You know, Artie," I finally say when I see him holding the carved wooden dog from the package under the tree, "I think we should close the book on that part of our lives."

And after it's out there, strung between us like a barbed-wire fence, I feel a lot lighter.

He looks straight at me and I see how all the west coast fog has lifted, leaving two black holes where his eyes should be. His jaw flexes as he tries to control his expression and then his fist crashes into the wall. "You just don't want to have my kid!" he yells.

"It's not that I don't want your kid, Artie," I say. "I'm not sure I want a kid at all." Better and better now. Cleansed.

But not for Artie. He can't know—doesn't want to know—and I start to understand how we're two very different people.

"What the fuck did we come down here for, Shawn? What were you thinking of when you said you wanted to come with me?"

"Artie—"

"Did you just come for the free ride?" he sneers. I can tell he's scared but doesn't know how to say so. And suddenly Sheila's right there in front of me again, pulling me into the mist with her. I have to struggle to stay here with Artie and that's when I realize I'm lost, unsure of where home is.

"You never have loved me, have you?" Artie grabs my arms, wanting to pull me back into the fight, so I shake my head, sad but not denying, and he raves as his fingers pinch the soft flesh above my elbows. "Well, you're no screaming catch, either, you know!" I nod in agreement as Sheila's eyes turn into that fishbowl look again and I smile, thinking how life has a funny way of leaving us behind as it works things out.

"Oh, it's funny, is it? Well, fuck you too, Shawn. Fuck you too!" As he leaves, he slams the door so hard that the moulding cracks.

That night I dream of northern rains and mountain streams, silver water bouncing off my face in slow-motion beads, long drinks of smooth
coldness reaching down inside me, my face reflected in the ripples of
river running over ice age granite. I wake, hot and sticky and alone in
the bed, the temperate climate of a California winter too mild for the
down comforter on top of me. I kick the cover onto the floor, too hot to
understand that it's not the heat that niggles me awake. The oven-like
dark feels claustrophobic, suffocating.

A keening noise slips through the open window and slides across my
damp skin, leaving goose-bumps. I shiver, temperature dropping and
sleep leaving as the mournful sound repeats and I hold onto that dark
California night. I wait, and the stillness of the valley is broken once
again by the donkey's sad bleat floating over the miles of quiet.

The braying increases as I lie, rolled onto my side now, face towards the window. I open my mouth, breathe in through clenched
teeth—"Eee"—out through a slack jaw—"awww," softly, trying to
communicate. The digital clock slips red numbers past my eyes and
sometime later the sky lightens, like a Christmas Eve over Bethlehem,
all starry and blue and night. After a while, I slide from the bed and go
to the window, drawn by the new moon and the cicadas in the empty
shadows of the garden. I listen hard and then, from across the dark distance, the slow and tentative aria of that vigilant donkey begins again.
His bray drifts toward me, lifting through the air like a night choir, and
I whisper back, wishing I could go to his side, feel his whiskered ears
against my cheek as I croon in response.

Artie doesn't come home until the next afternoon and when he arrives,
he sits outside, passenger in a classmate's Volkswagen, talking. When I
look out the window, I see him, hand on his brow, and her, hand on his
cheek. I close the blinds against the hot California sun and sigh.

"It's a new day, Artie," I smile when he comes through the door, hag-
gard and drained. But the fog is back in his eyes, the eyes I loved so
well up north.

He doesn't move so I go to him, take his hands and stand before him, staring into all that grey.

"Come for a walk?"

He nods, and somewhere in the distance I hear a braying aria.

We walk in a field of wildflowers by the river, the lanky palms and eucalyptus throwing shadows like fly rods. When we sit in the middle of a clearing, a cloud of butterflies lifts around us like a flock of birds. Artie holds out his hand and a big black one with white spots and turquoise dabs on its wings lands on his palm, fluttering briefly. We watch for a few minutes while it lies next to the warmth of his skin. Then its wings close together, shutting like an old suitcase, and it dies. Artie holds onto it but I look away, that parched feeling rising inside me again. And as I turn my head, I see them everywhere, their wings fluttering among the grass and flowers all around us, coming home to die.

I walk back through the dense scream of greenery along the riverbank, scattering Sheila's memory as I go. With each discard, a part of me passes over to this land and I am released to its spell.

Later I write home again:

"Artie's coming home next month, bringing a memento from me. I'm going to stay a while, at the place in the enclosed photos. The animals and the river will be my company for now. The donkey has become a special friend—she likes to sing so I named her Tosca—but the cat and the goat are growing on me too. You'll understand if you come visit."

I put the butterfly in a little box with tissue paper all around it so its wings won't break. It's the first time I've ever touched a dead thing and I hope they don't mind that I'm sending them a corpse. I hope they'll know that it's good for me to do this, to send something from the south, from home.

The Possibility of Jack

Marie's friend Jack is trying to seduce her, doing things that make his intentions entirely clear. This has been going on since last summer—almost a year now, Marie realizes.

Jack is always giving things, bringing things, to her. He seems to want to fulfill some archaic image of man-as-provider and it makes her feel as though she is supposed to play a role too, to blush at his ardour or to swoon at a mere glance from him. It annoys her that she always ends up giving Jack her full attention in payment for his unwarranted gifts.

Sometimes Marie wishes she could just dismiss him with a sharp warning: "Piss off, Jack—I'm not interested!" But they'd grown up together, gone to school and university together, and, when eventually they commiserated over individually failed marriages together, Marie discovered a kind of intellectual kinship that she hadn't been aware of before. Now when they talk—when he doesn't want something from her that she can't give—Marie feels aligned with Jack, attuned to his way of thinking. At those times she finds herself re-evaluating his presence in her life and then she grows confused about whether she wants to be more than long-time friends.

If they'd been lovers, it would be easy to accept his repeated attempts to woo her, but Marie can't see Jack in a sexual light. It's like trying to imagine bedding Santa Claus, his fatherly beard, the crinkles around his eyes, a well-rounded belly. Nothing stirs in her nether regions; there is no hot rush between her legs or her ribs whenever she considers him. But Marie isn't stupid: she knows that thirty-five years of friendship is worth more than most marriages these days.

Jack and Marie do the kind of things that married couples do. Or at least the things done by married couples who enjoy each other. Hiking, sailing, skiing, dancing, cooking.

Last summer they went on a canoe trip of the Powell Lakes. In Vancouver, before they left, Marie had been scared, but also yearning to go. To be in the wilderness again.

They took the dogs, his and hers, and went into the pristine quiet of the forest around the lakes, their world on their backs. Marie's terrier raced up the trails in frantic excitement while Jack's labrador padded along in patient attendance.

"Mutt and Jeff," Jack had remarked. Marie had thought he was referring to him and her.

"Aw, you're not a mutt—just a purebred in disguise!" she jibed.

The August heat was blazing and Jack came off the lake each day with a deeper shade of tan. As the pallid city boy receded, Marie found herself looking at him in a different light. He was fit and healthy, despite his beefy figure, and she liked the fact that he was outdoorsy, contemplative, financially secure—traits similar to her own. For a brief afternoon, Marie closed her eyes against the August sun and dreamed about taking her friendship with Jack to another place. What she wanted was something bigger, more consuming than an easy companionship. But the face in her dream was not Jack's, and so when Marie opened her eyes, she dismissed her idea with a grim smile. They were good friends and she didn't want to complicate things with unrealistic expectations.

The trip took on a rhythm and a life of its own, whole days of visual splendour unfolding one after another. They rose early, while the air was still mild, swam in the warm, mirror-still water, eating breakfast between the trees and the shore, waiting for the sun to burst over the black hills around them. During the paddle to the next portage, periods of quiet strokes were interrupted with serious philosophical discussion or, sometimes, jokes that filled the emptiness with their startling laughter. Marie felt swollen with happiness, freed by the knowledge that their common history made such a trip possible, without overtones of expectation.

Sometimes they stopped in the afternoons to swim or fish, lie on the rocks and read. At night by the fire they relived old events or discussed new directions in their lives, and in the silences they listened to the plaintive loons on the lake. Looking at the horizon, Marie was content to see the years she and Jack had spent together melt into one long memory.

On the fourth day out, they went for an evening walk along the trail from their campsite, found a hewn-out log facing the sunset. They sat together enjoying the feeling of being in a painting, small figures at the corner of a large canvas.

And then, "I'm really interested in you, Marie," spilled into the quiet dusk and the muscles in her neck seized. She fought her impulse to run into the fading day, stayed and felt the gigantic silence between them. A loon crying out to its lost mate, noisy and alone in the middle of the lake, swam circles in the dying light. Marie focused on the loon, the bird's need so loud he couldn't hear the silence all around.

The daylight ended steadily and Jack spoke again: "What are you thinking?"

"I wish you hadn't said that."

From the periphery of her view, Marie saw Jack's head turn away from her, bowing to look at his hands clasped between his legs, foot tracing patterns in the dirt.

"Look, Marie—we've known each other since kindergarten. We have a lot of history together, and the last few days we've shared a lot of fun. It's easy to be with you and I thought ... I guess I just wanted to let you know that." He picked up a rock and flung it into the distance.

It was too dark to see where it landed, but Marie heard the plock of rock entering water.

Then she felt Jack's hand reaching for hers. She squeezed it quickly and let go, stood up.

"Let's go back and light a fire—it's getting cold."

"Okay. But don't be upset about this, all right?"

"I'm not," she lied.

Marie didn't know she had lied until she felt the knot growing in her neck on the way back to camp. She didn't know how to dissolve her fear and for a moment she wished she could make Jack disappear, like the rock in the water, covered over by darkness.

Marie hung over the edge of the canoe, peering into the depths of the lake. Near the shore she'd been able to see the bottom, but out here in the middle of the water there was nothing more than her imagination to suggest bottom. She wondered if the eerie hint of dark floating shapes was because of her fear of monsters or the rays of sharp sunlight making images of floating particles in the water. Every so often a deadhead covered in slimy algae would appear, poking up out of the dusty depths, pointing at her like a finger. She was supposed to warn Jack if any of the deadheads were sharp enough or close enough to the surface that they needed to paddle around them. But he was paddling so slowly this morning that she wasn't worried.

"Marie?"

"Mmhmm?" She hoped her warm laziness would influence whatever Jack had to say.

"Can we talk some more about last night?"

Marie closed her eyes. Water, water everywhere.

"I'm not sure I have much to say about it, Jack."

"I'd sure like to know how you're feeling."

Marie picked up her paddle, began stroking the smooth water beside her, stirring up hard ripples. "You're my friend, Jack. I like you for my friend. I don't want to change anything."

"I don't either, Marie. But I'd like us to be closer if we can."

"That's what I'm saying, Jack. I don't think we can be closer without being physical and I don't want that."

"Is there a particular reason you aren't interested?"

Marie let the silence build around the sound of the paddles dipping and sifting through the water. She bit her lip, trying for the words that would tell Jack she wasn't attracted to him that way. She wanted to end this trip, get out of this canoe and still have Jack for a friend.

"I don't want a lover, Jack. I'm happy being single and having lots of solitary time. My life is very full, even hectic. There's no room for someone else in it."

"One night a week?"

"Yes. I mean no! There are lots of weeks where one night a week is too much—I don't always have the time!"

"Well, on those weeks you could tell me if you're too busy and I could do something else."

Marie could feel the ridges of tension building along her shoulders, the ache from the pull of her paddle, the dampness under her arms, the exertion of all her energy. And now her eyes burned too.

"I don't want to be committed to anything or anybody, Jack. I want to concentrate on pulling back and focusing on my life right now."

"Does that mean we could try again later?"

"Let me think about it, okay?"

"I understand—okay."

The tears stung Marie's sunburned cheeks and she stopped her furious paddling to wipe her nose. She was glad she had her back to Jack, glad she couldn't see his good intentions.

That evening she doused her coffee with an extra shot of Southern Comfort. It helped her get to sleep, but later she found herself awake and claustrophobic. She climbed over the two dogs to unzip the tent door.

"You okay?" Jack mumbled from inside his sleeping bag.

"Fine—I'm fine. Just have to pee," Marie whispered into the opening as she closed the fly behind her. Outside the dark was so complete that she froze, listening to small scufflings in the bush. After a minute, the night noises and the blackness grew familiar and the lunging shapes on the trees became towels swinging in the night. Marie curled her blanket around her shoulders and hunched up against a trunk to stare at the lake.

A loon paraded close to shore with erratic zigzags of head and wake. Marie watched the bird, admiring the reflection of moonlight on its spotted back, imagining she could see the glint of its black eye looking at her. She remembered reading about First Nations' youths being sent into the forest to find their spirit guides, their totems, and wondered if this loon might be hers.

The loon tacked across the still lake in frantic search of something. Whenever it dived, Marie closed her eyes, trying to feel the pulse of dark water in her ears, imagining the underwater sounds of fish, maybe, or insects. But when the loon surfaced, Marie could see nothing in its beak, could only guess where it had been. Not even a sheen of wetness remained on its back, as if the water had not touched the bird streaking through the blackness.

It made her think about how wanting something too much can obsess a person, and about how Jack wanted something she didn't want. She didn't see how Jack's desire could be forgotten or even allowed to fade without affecting their friendship. It felt as though his need was always going to hang over her so that, whenever she looked at him, Marie would remember the stifling feeling of being close to him in the canoe, the tent, the water.

At dawn, Marie uncurled herself from the blanket to swim in the coloured water. The envelope of warm waves against her nakedness soothed the rawness of the night. She swam away from the shore, into the middle of the lake, and when she turned to look back at the campsite, she felt the caress of the hot sun on her head out of water. Removed from the shadow of Jack's longing, Marie felt less disposed to be angry with him. She wanted to be kind, not hurtful. After all, he was her friend, her old friend.

She saw Jack's bulky shape moving about the campsite, saw him setting up the camp stove to make coffee. He flung the remains of last night's coffee into the campfire ashes, then trudged down to the water's edge to fill the pot. Marie was treading water, waiting for him to notice her. He turned, walked back up the slope to the picnic table. Marie put her face into the water and swam with slow, definite strokes towards the rock where her clothes lay.

"Hey!" Jack's voice, fuzzy from sleep, croaked when he heard her come up the slope. "Where were you?"

Marie towelled her hair as she walked towards him. She sat down at the table, a spot in the sun. "Out there. I waved at you when you were peeing ... didn't you see me?"

Jack's eyes widened in surprise, a reaction that intrigued Marie. She bent over, let her hair fall forward, rubbed the wet undersides of her head, waiting for him to call her bluff. But Jack said nothing, turning to busy himself instead with the knotted food bag. Marie looked at him through the curtain of hair over her eyes, watched as he buried his arm in the canvas bag, groping about in fierce concentration. She could feel his tight silence and realized, without understanding, that she had made him uncomfortable.

"Jack," she sat up and flung her hair back, intending to put him at ease.

"Yeah?"

Jack's shirt stretched across his broad back and Marie waited for his shoulders to turn. When they didn't, Marie changed her mind. "Do you want porridge for breakfast?" she asked instead.

"I guess. Yeah, sure."

They listened to the coffee bubble and hiss while they ate. The lake, and Marie, shimmered, calm, under the glare of morning sun.

It was well after summer, the air deepening into autumn sharpness, when Marie felt enough distance to think about the canoe trip with any pleasure. The end of the trip had been irritating, a long, drawn-out summary to a foregone conclusion. Jack's neurotic idiosyncracies—an insistence on packing things in a certain manner and a specific order—had forced Marie to relinquish her calm. Whenever she talked to him, the sight of gentle longing in his eyes caused a sharp edge to creep into her voice. In the evenings, to have some time alone and regain a sense of self, Marie had encouraged Jack to go fishing, leaving her with the dogs and the sunset and giving her time to plan how, when they rested along a portage, she could keep him from massaging her tired back muscles.

Of course she'd had to hug him goodbye at the end of the trip, and she'd done it without care, untangling herself quickly from Jack's confining arms. But tonight, feeling the arctic air drifting down from the mountains and through the glass panes of the windows, Marie thinks of the grey of west coast winter, the long afternoons and black nights to come. She thinks about Jack's invitation to call him any time, and she wonders if she was wrong, too hasty, to push him away. The possibility of Jack—of any man—in her bed is enticing and Marie doesn't want to consider the repercussions.

She goes to her bedroom and stands in front of the mirror, turning sideways to look at her profile. She pokes at the gentle bulge that is her abdomen. Her hands push at either side of the slackness, bunching the fat into a doughnut shape, bellybutton in the centre. She shakes her head.

Absolutely disgusting. Last year I still looked okay in a bathing suit, but not now. Not any more.

Her eyes move upwards and she leans into the mirror, checking for new wrinkles around the eyes and mouth. Even her face betrays her, sagging into blobs around the eyes, jowls at the jawline. *Forty-two and my life is over: how can I ever be sexual again?*

It's true, she is not centrefold material any longer. But Jack still wants her. It might work. If she could let it.

Marie sighs, turns from the bleak vision in the mirror and slumps into her favourite armchair, closing her eyes. When they open again, she is looking at the phone. She wills it to ring, waits for the sound, then sighs and gets up. She crosses the room, dials the number she has known for years.

Marie spends an hour putting on makeup. Not that she has to look a certain way for Jack, but so that she feels a certain way about herself. For a while it works: Marie is calm and capable when Jack arrives. But later, at a singles bar, Jack starts talking about the two of them again, resurrecting the possibility of being a couple in a relationship.

"I think it's important to know what turns your partner on, don't you?" he says from across the table.

"I think that's the kind of thing you discover about someone as you get to know them," she answers.

"What about asking, though, so you can experiment together?"

"Feels too cold and calculated to me."

"You wouldn't like to be asked?"

"I guess that would depend who was asking, Jack."

"If it was me? If we were ever to get together?"

Marie feels the anxiety—his stubbornness—shoved in her face like an iron cell door. She pleads allergies to the smoke in the air and goes to the ladies' room. She knows that Jack will call for the bill while she's gone. He will hurry to pay before she gets back, holding his wallet close to his chest as though to protect it from muggers—or from being emptied. She is glad to avoid that scene: she would have to look down, away, to hide her embarrassment with Jack's lack of finesse. She is uncomfortable that she costs him anything at all, that he never lets her pay. It feels like she is providing a kind of service, prostitution of a lesser degree.

They go to Jack's place. He wants to play her his new CD of Gaelic jigs. Marie hopes the music will break the funk she has slipped into, but Jack's apartment is like an animal's den, grease spatters all over the stove, dust as thick as a layer of topsoil so that mess seems to sprout from it.... She squeezes herself against the arm of the couch, sits with knees tightly crossed and stiff back. Now everything crowds her: the way Jack is dressed—his clothes as though they have lain in a wrinkled heap all night—his portly body, his always easygoing nature. Suddenly she has to go home. Not feeling well, she tells him, and Jack helps her with her coat.

In the car Marie takes deep breaths of air, like stiff snorts of brandy, to calm herself. She feels a reckless anger building inside and she wants to tell Jack to look in a mirror, see himself.

"Even semi-greatness requires attention to details," Marie wants to say. "You have a lot of skills but you need to dig deep and find a path, a career—something other than me to devote yourself to."

Instead, after a while she asks, "How was your interview last week?" and Jack answers in the way she expects.

"Oh, fine. But the guy I talked with seemed unclear about what he was looking for, whether they could use my expertise or not."

"So when do you expect to hear back from them?"

"Well, actually I thought I'd've heard something by now."

"Are you going to call them back, check it out?"

"No. I figure if they don't call me, it means they're not interested."

Marie turns to glare out her window. The rain begins as Jack's car approaches her block. Marie shakes her head, trying to imagine herself and Jack lumped under the covers, her sagging stomach against another bulge of unfamiliar origin. If she gave in to her physical desires and the experience turned out to be like a stuttering teenage foray into the world of passion—slobbering, perspiring, unfulfilling sex, insubstantial and immemorable or—worse—all too memorable—how would she dismiss him then? Jack, she knew, would want to stay for breakfast the next morning, would want to talk about how wonderful last night had been.

He might suggest moving in, making pancakes and eggs for her in the morning. The quiet calm of first light filled with coffee and muted dogs barking in the distance would have to be relinquished. Instead there would be Jack, too attentive for her to slip away, wanting her full concentration, and so earnest that she must listen. He would bury her with his blatant desire; she would become invisible, even to him.

Marie slips out of the car when it stops at the curb. "Good night, Jack," she bends to say before shutting the door. "Thanks."

She hurries up the path to her door, then slows and sighs. She's forgotten to leave the porch light on and she has to dig to find her keys at the bottom of her purse. Jack's car is still waiting at the curb, the engine coughing as though sick with the flu. Marie's hand closes around the key ring and she unlocks the door, turning in the flood of light from the hallway to wave goodbye. As Jack's car pulls away, a dark shape appears at the end of the walkway.

Marie recognizes the heavy, rolling movement of the figure. Mrs.

Grapelli. Marie reaches inside the open door to turn on the porch light and an old woman materializes from behind the silhouette of bushes and shadows, moving stiffly with the help of a cane.

Marie can hear the old woman's wheezing as she approaches the stairs. She stops at the bottom, tips her head sideways to the light. Like a robin, Marie thinks.

"Is ... this ...?" The old woman's voice is thin, so sparse that Marie leans in close to answer.

"Marie, Mrs. Grapelli. You've got the wrong house. Shall I walk you home?"

Ancient eyes stare without focus. Good lord—why is she out here in the dark?

"Please ..." The woman wheezes.

Marie descends the wooden stairs, takes old Mrs. Grapelli's arm and turns her gently, heads slowly back up the walkway.

The old woman takes small, shuffling steps and Marie has to pause several times to encourage her along. She studies the bent crone, amazed and somewhat repulsed by her advanced age. She sees the blue wateriness of the skin on the back of her neighbour's hand, the pronounced curve of her shoulders hunched over the cane. And the painstaking effort of her breath, so weak and with such gasping sounds.

At the house next door, Marie hands the old woman over to her granddaughter, a tired young mother harassed by her non-stop care duties.

At home again, Marie stands behind the closed door. There was, after all, the matter of companionship in life. Who will check on her when she is elderly? She has no one, no husband or child. What if she becomes like old Mrs. Grapelli, bent and blind, wandering city streets at night, dependent on horrified strangers to pick her up when she slips and falls on old, splintery bones?

The next morning the city lies beneath the pressure of iron-grey skies. A wet snow begins to fall while Marie sits at her desk. Her eyes are drawn to the waft of snowflakes dancing sleepily outside the window. She gets up to light a fire and take a break from marking the pile of student exams brought home for the Christmas break. Crouched by the fireplace, she lets herself be mesmerized by the crackling flames.

When the phone rings, Marie leaps to answer it. The thought of human contact, if only at the end of a telephone line, is reassuring.

"Guess who?" says Jack.

"Hi, Jack. I'm just sitting down to work."

"Okay—I won't take long. I forgot to tell you last night that I finally took the film from our trip to be developed and I just got it back. Thought you might like to see the prints?"

"Yes—yes I would. Are they any good?"

"Well, the ones of the dogs are the best!"

"Figures!"

"What about tomorrow? What are you doing in the morning?"

"Tomorrow's good. About ten?"

"Sounds great."

"Come in," Marie opens the door wide. "You want a coffee? I just made some."

"Sure." Jack beams at her. "Love some. Here"—he holds out an envelope—"I brought you a Christmas card."

"*Is that a candy cane in your pocket,*" it asks on the outside, and inside, "*Or are you just glad to see me?*"

"Nice taste!" Marie remarks without looking at him.

Inside the card there is also a handwritten inscription:

> *Roses are red*
> *Violets are blue*
> *Why don't you come for dinner Saturday night*
> *for some lamb vindaloo?*
> *Then we can take all our clothes off*
> *And I'll kiss, nibble and lick you!*

The panic rises in her chest and Marie turns aside. She feels Jack's eyes watching her, reading her. She holds on to the counter with her empty hand and laughs, hoping it doesn't sound too hollow. She turns around. "I'll have to censor these last two lines in case anyone else reads the card!"

"You like my proposition?"

Into the blur swims Marie's loon, the crying bird of last summer. She hears the loon's loud need, the lake's waiting silence. She watches it dive, traces its body streaking like a dark rock, beak pointed at the lake's bottom, weaving to miss the deadheads. She holds her breath, waiting for the solitary bird to surface, to see if he's found anything. Anything at all.

The silence is drowning her, choking any possibility of words in the small passage of air from her chest. She stands next to Jack, her willing mate, trying to think. Trying to try.

Maybe she should.... If it doesn't work, she could tell him later....

He puts his arm around her shoulder, stands next to her against the kitchen counter. It was the *good night* and *thank you* that always seemed to mean something else at the end of a night. At least that would stop.... If she did....

"Earth to Marie," Jack speaks into her ear.

The intensity that permeates anything Jack does or says, that depletes her and leaves her wanting to hide. The rocks, the water.

"What's going on in there, Marie? Don't shut me out." The arm on her shoulder holds her against him and Marie feels herself being pulled under. She struggles to keep her head above the water, musters a smile.

"Sorry, Jack. Not all here, I guess."

"That's okay." The cupped palm around her shoulder, gripping. "I'm here for you, you know."

Jack bends his face over Marie's, his eyes so close she shuts hers against them. It must seem like acquiescence and he reaches his mouth to hers. Her neck tenses at the first tickle of moustache. Jack's other arm pulls her round and into him. Marie tries to steer her way through the deadheads with her eyes closed. The rush of water against her ears.

Do You Remember?

Peter Welsh was the first boy I ever kissed. He was the fastest run-
ner in the class, which gave him a rank of importance in grade
six. It also made him an object of the twelve-year-old female
fantasy. My peer group ogled Peter's bulging calves and biceps during
PE class and described him as *cute*, a derivative without merit but with
a message of yearning behind it. So when Peter started paying a lot of
attention to me, there was an instant rise in my social status. It started
me wondering about the boy-girl thing and gave me something to feel
anxious about. And when, one rainy recess, Peter and I were left alone
beneath a dripping tree—our crowd of friends sprinting across the field
as if in secret agreement—the sound of the bell interrupted the rough
squeeze that Peter surprised my hand with.

"Wait for me after school," he commanded. "I got something to
tell you."

The afternoon was a blurred stretch of time, of enduring the repetitve

71

circuitry of my thoughts and of waiting for the bell that would begin my future. Would he ask me to marry him? Should we elope? How could we meet without the whispered giggles of my friends and his? Should I tell my mother I was staying late to help Mr. Hamilton?

"I can't walk home with you today," I told my best friend Nancy. "I have to go to the dentist after school."

Nancy seemed surprised but unperturbed about finding a substitute for my company that afternoon and her nonchalance deflated the huge importance of my secret. I needn't have bothered withholding the truth. As Peter and I emerged from the strictly off-limits woods surrounding the postwar schoolhouse, a group of boys awaited his news, the impatience of curiosity shining in their eyes. We parted company and at school the next day, I was the topic of many discussions.

"I thought you had to go to the dentist," Nancy taunted.

"Next week. I made a mistake."

"Or was it someone else who wanted to inspect your mouth!" Nancy snickered conspiratorially and ran off laughing with her new friend on her arm. I wasn't sure whether I was left alone because of envy or because of a flaw in my character.

Peter and I arranged "chance" meetings at a mutual friend's house—often my neighbour, another classmate—and stared at each other with the dewy gaze of cows chewing their cud, making sarcastic, teasing comments as substitute for exploring the dark, steamy environment of that mysterious world known as adulthood. It was one of those beginnings that later in life are referred to as obvious. As in obviously impossible.

"Boys, choose your partners for the Red River Waltz."

The line of Brylcreemed and brush-cut heads flexed and split as the boys aimed for the wall of girls across the varnished gym floor. Mrs. Wright, the after-school dance teacher, stood on the stage and supervised the partnering.

"Peter Welsh, you go back to the boys' side and start again. No running!"

I watched him turn away as Robbie Turner loomed in front of me.

"Wanna dance, Gail?"

I started to shake my head but saw him glance up at the stage. Mrs. Wright was Robbie's aunt and the hard glint that blinded me—whether from the reflection of ceiling lights on the highly varnished floor or the glare of Mrs. Wright's rhinestone-framed glasses, I wasn't sure—made me shrug in submission. Robbie reached for my hand and I winced as his sweaty paw closed around my fingers.

"Form four lines and get ready for the opening bars."

Robbie's eyes were level with my newly sprouted breasts and I stared over the top of his head. Peter had his back to me but I saw his shoulders shake with laughter and his partner, Suzanne Durham, swell with a blush of conquest.

Mrs. Wright removed her glasses as she bent over the school phonograph. Static crackled from the loudspeakers on either side of the stage and we took our positions, arms extended in an awkward imitation of grace. We turned our eyes to the stage and watched Mrs. Wright adjusting the sweater clip on her cardigan before holding out her arms to an invisible partner. In the golden shower of stage lights, she was transformed from an aging dance teacher to a fairytale vision, and we held our breath, waiting below her in the still, cold air of the gymnasium, a sweaty, pubescent class of senior dance students. Then, as the static died and a sudden silence announced the imminent burst of music, Mrs. Wright turned to look over her shoulder at us, arms and smile poised.

"On the count of three, girls begin with the left foot, boys with the right. And one, and two and THREE!"

Our awkward bodies lurched into the dance, step-counting our way around the floor and keeping pace with Vera Wright, 1951 Arkansas Waltz Champion.

Mrs. Wright may have had it in mind to recreate her past in us. Certainly she took great pains to teach us the rigid code of personal grooming and presentation that she herself followed. It was one of the reasons, she liked to tell us, that she'd been so successful in her career.

"Do you suppose I could've won a beauty queen title as well as all those dance championships if I'd been lazy about my appearance, boys and girls?" Mrs. Wright queried us. And, whenever our efforts at grooming resulted in noticeable slips, she pointed out the pitfalls of slovenliness: "Those who forget about the importance of looking their best are soon ignored themselves, children."

The result of her inspirational lectures was that, after two years of first junior and then intermediate ballroom lessons, all of us in the senior class knew that there was a certain protocol to be followed before presenting ourselves on the dance floor. Socks must be wrinkle-free, hair must be combed and hands washed before allowing ourselves to be viewed by potential partners. These ablutions were often supervised by Vera Wright herself.

"Never, never let them see you looking anything less than perfect, girls." She circulated among us in the change room, primping a crinoline here, a hair bow there.

The boys received a similar lecture, the focus in their room on behaviour.

"Now remember, boys—only gentlemen are admitted into society. You must always be alert to your best manners when you're with a lady. What does this mean, Peter?"

"Um, you open the door for her and help her on with her coat. And bow before and after a dance."

"And Jeremy—I hope you've been paying attention—where must you never, ever let your fingers be?"

"In yer nose, Miz Wright."

"I think we're ready."

We climbed the stairs from those basement change rooms in a flurry of anticipation, sometimes with new shoes or dresses to show off, other times with new hairstyles or jewellery, and stood facing the stage at attention, ready for the final inspection.

And Mrs. Wright would bend and peer at us from her pedestal, searching for any hint of imperfection amongst her trainees.

"James, your fingernails need cleaning. Go fix them, right now. And Carmela, you haven't brushed your hair, have you? Off you go. And while we're waiting for those two, boys and girls, we'll review the polka. Find yourself a space on the floor...."

The two infractors would slink away, our eyes following them until Mrs. Wright called us back to attention. Then she would turn her back to us, her thin frame straining at the filmy weightlessness of her gown as she held up her arms and stood like the Statue of Liberty, waiting.

"I can still hear someone moving," she'd murmur. The rustle of petticoats and the shuffle of feet would cease. And she'd begin.

"Like the waltz, but with the extra little hop, remember? One, two, three—hop! One, two, three...."

Mrs. Wright held an annual showcase of her students' talent on Parents' Night. She had no need of advertising for new students—she'd taught most of my friends' and neighbours' older siblings and was well known to local families—but the showcase was the highlight of the year towards which she, and we, worked. Every step, every curtsy, every brushed curl was intended for that one moment in the spotlight when the best of us had an opportunity to demonstrate what we'd learned.

It was on the evening of our senior dance showcase that I first became aware of my changing future.

Peter was partnered with Suzanne and I was partnered with Mrs. Wright's nephew, Robbie, for the Virginia Reel, a dance I loved because of the high-spirited music and the fast-paced stepping. Mrs. Wright had made us short skirts that flared above the waist when our partners spun us. The boys wore red satin cummerbunds to match our red skirts and the flash of red and black from the stage looked hot and fiery. The music blared above the fold-up metal seats of the audience below us and we stepped and whirled and promenaded and do-si-doed and then Robbie tripped on his shoelace and lost his place in the allemande. I kept going, thinking he'd catch up and then it was the final promenade. As the dance ended, I looked up to find Peter had become my partner.

"I'd like to kiss you," he hissed into my ear during the applause. And, as Mrs. Wright gave her speech of thanks, he squeezed my waist. Instead of fading, the flush of heat on my face deepened until it matched Peter's cummerbund.

Perhaps Vera Wright was too old, too lost in the dreams of her past to understand what she was doing. Her children had grown and left long ago, as had her husband, though no one seemed to know whether he'd died or run off with someone else. Maybe he'd found a partner who knew how to be close without having to dance; someone who didn't have to have her hair and makeup done before he approached. When I remember Mrs. Wright now, I picture her swaying across an empty stage, lilting strains of bygone music wafting around her like the skirt of her dance dress. In that image her arms are always extended, always open and waiting to be filled by some substance of solidity.

The dance showcase was an annual event held just before Easter holidays. Until then, the only way for Peter and I to avoid the teasing of school-mates was to find somewhere to be alone during recess and lunch.

One day after school he approached me and whispered, "Let's go into the woods."

I looked over his shoulder at my friends retreating in the distance, at Peter's friends openly giggling and pointing at us, stalled on the open playground.

"C'mon." He slipped his hand into mine and pulled me towards the leafy undergrowth at the edge of the playing field. I hung back at first, afraid of being caught for going out of bounds. My eyes searched the playground for the supervising teacher, but when Peter's hand tugged again, I followed him into the forbidden forest. He stopped suddenly and I bumped into him, his face right in front of mine. A well of black emptiness opened and I shut my eyes as his lips closed in on me.

The surroundings and atmosphere of that momentous first kiss are lost to me now. I picture a rain-soaked alder grove, the damp rub of bark on my coat when Peter coralled me against a trunk with his ski-jacketed arms. His mat of moist hair against my cheek, the smell of boyness, wet and woodsy, shoved into my nostrils as our hands rubbed at each other's backs, nervous and unfeeling. We had waited, gathering courage to take this giant step, wanting to end our virginal status but scared, too, of the finality in crossing that line. As the skin of Peter's cheek lifted against mine, I kept my eyes closed against the possibility of recognizing, in his eyes, the failure of the event. Two quilted bodies pressed close together beneath a brutal crush of cracked lips and inside those ski jackets nothing but panting hearts, slowing once the anxiety of anticipation was over. It was nothing at all like the descriptions of passion in the Nurse Nancy books I'd found in the library.

When Peter's brother told him about French kissing, I expressed horror at the thought of intermingling tongues and germs and spit. But we were entering high school in the fall so we spent longer periods of time in the woods, practising.

We began to talk about sex—about hard-ons and beavers—the only way we knew how.

"I've got a boner for you," said the note he passed me in class one day. And when I leaned forward to look across the rows at him, Peter grinned and pointed at the exercise book lying face down in his lap.

We wondered about our parents having sex or whether they were too old.

"Well, I guess Mrs. Wright doesn't do it, anyway!" I was proud of myself for figuring that one out.

"Why not?"

"Well, she hasn't got a husband to do it with."

"What about old Penis-breath? You never seen them together?"

"Mr. Hamilton?" Peter didn't know our teacher was married?

Peter held up his left hand, thumb and forefinger forming a circle. He lay the forefinger of his right hand inside the circle and slid it in and out suggestively. "And I bet they do more than that, too!" He laughed and the harshness of the sound made my shoulders tighten, but I only nudged him in pretend shock.

Homework was an excuse to call each other and Peter and I talked on the phone, two neophytes bantering back and forth, until his mother or mine told us it was time to get off. If he told me he was going to be at my neighbour's on the weekend, I'd find an excuse to go next door, sitting on the driveway and watching while Peter and Fred built a go-cart or some other boy-thing. Often, Peter would dance around Fred, poking and jabbing at him until he agreed to a wrestling match that I was supposed to judge. Watching them roll and tumble, putting knees and hands in places where they could hurt each other, I knew that Mrs. Wright would disapprove. But when Peter sat up afterwards, I made the kind of admiring comment I was sure she'd have encouraged.

"Shouldn't you be careful of Fred when you're so much stronger?" And I'd whisper it so Fred's feelings weren't hurt. Peter would shrug carelessly, but there was a flush of pride in his eyes when he turned away.

During the summer, Peter and I regularly visited the fort he and his friends had built in the woods. We necked sitting up, heads and shoulders pushed together like two pieces of sculpture welded into some implausible position. And Peter's hands would slide, two tenuous vines, up and down and around my trunk. After each dizzying afternoon in those shadow-dappled woods, I left in a growing state of breathlessness, the boy-girl thing increasingly muddied in my mind.

Over the previous winter an incident had occurred to instigate the off-limits ban on the woods. Somewhere in that deep stretch of green leafiness, horrific deeds had been perpetrated on a younger school girl. Afterwards, during the dark December mornings and darker afternoons of that last elementary winter, most of the girls were driven regularly to and from the school in order to avoid proximity to the woods and any recurrence of the incident.

From the back seat of my parents' Chevrolet, I had stared as the old coupe slid heavily past the place where my childhood memories were vested, looking in wonder at the beckoning reaches of those familiar trees and trying to imagine the tangible threat that now existed where once we'd lived out our fantasies. Admonished never again to walk home alone in the dark, to always have a parent or an older student go with us if we had to walk, or to ask a neighbour for a ride, the woods had seemed lost to me forever.

"You're starting to grow up, now," was the explanation given in response to our puzzled *whys*. The adult eyes would slide away from ours as if to signal there remained nothing more to say about this sudden change in life.

And soon thereafter we were herded into a basement room of the school for a film called *Your Changing Bodies*.

"Now that you are becoming women, there are things you must be careful about." The nurse's bright eyes swept across the tops of our heads as we sat, fidgeting and wondering why just we and none of the boys had been allowed to miss arithmetic for a movie. "Especially when some of you start to go with boys," Nurse continued, "you need to be aware. Some girls"—her eyes swept over us in the other direction—"have got into trouble by letting boys touch them in places they shouldn't."

I thought of Peter and how he'd asked to put his hand under my blouse and my shoulders sank a little against the back of my chair.

"Men have different needs from women, girls, a fact you must always remember when you start dating. If you have any concerns, you should speak with your mothers."

I thought of my mother and of what she would say if I told her what Peter and I had done. I hadn't wanted him to touch me at all but when I shied away, he told me what I already knew: married men and women did things like this all the time. So I closed my eyes and he lifted my blouse but the cold—or the anticipation—made my nipples shrivel and I pushed his hands away to cover myself.

"This film explains why you need to be more cautious now that you are growing up and it will help you to understand some of the changes that are coming. After we've watched it, we can talk about any of the things you don't understand or anything else you're curious about."

The film showed time-lapse animations of sprouting breasts and pubic hair and then it diagrammed what would happen inside us: tubes sweeping eggs from the ovaries into the ripening uterus before whisking everything neatly away, beyond the person of the girl-cum-woman. We talked about boys and someone asked about male organs and Nurse told us it was natural to feel curious about their bodies.

"But don't ever let a boy talk you into doing what you don't like."
Nurse frowned at us. "And remember: you can get into trouble day or
night."

In an instant the relief manufactured at the memory of Peter's hands
sweeping over me in the broadness of daylight dissolved. Suddenly
even the light of the coming summer dusk seemed deceptive, the soft
pools of lamplight accentuating growing shadows as I hurried home
from those trysts in the woods, unnerved by my recent knowledge of
boys and men with all their dark needs. Now I glanced about with new
anxiety whenever Peter and I entered the threatening interior and I
wondered how I'd lost my innocence.

There were some Fridays after dance class that mothers were late in
picking up their children. We waited in the quietness of the shadowy
gym while Mrs. Wright switched lights and checked the change rooms,
listening to the echo of dull sounds crashing like an avalanche in the
empty hall.

One Friday I was the last one waiting for my ride when Mr. Hamilton
came into the gym. He paused when he noticed me seated at the edge of
the stage, swinging my legs and staring dazedly at the floor.

"Had a good dance, Gail?" he asked me.

I nodded, unsure how to converse with my teacher outside the
classroom.

He smiled then, a brief, unconvincing movement of the lips, and
moved into the shadows at the back of the stage.

I turned my head surreptitiously, trying to follow his back into the
dim light but could see only the grotesque growth of his shadow as it
bent away from the light.

I peered at the clock on the opposite wall of the gym, saw the second
hand jerking steadily forward. 5:07.

I heard the murmur of voices behind me, blurred by the whisper-
ing rustle of Mrs. Wright's dress as she moved about. I looked at my
left hand folded over the edge of the stage and lifted it to check my
fingernails, tilting my head a little. I stared at the whites of my half-
moons with serious concern, becoming aware of the deafening silence

in the room. Hand clenched now, I strained for some evidence of the adults, wanting the reassurance of their company but also wanting my own presence to be unnoticed and forgotten. I let my hand drift down, leaning back into the dark at the edge of the stage and pushing myself beyond the rim of light until I too was swallowed by the shadows.

In the dark I saw a quick flash of light and recognized the lurid glow of Mr. Hamilton's wristwatch, familiar from all the occasions it had glazed across my desk. The reflective face moved downwards, falling hypnotically through the blackness, dropping then pausing, glinting cruelly before disappearing suddenly. Mrs. Wright's crinoline whispered in the quiet and I caught my breath at the sound of the starchy hiss. I peered into the depths of backstage, seeing a brief flash of ghostliness, the white of skin, and my spine pushed into the wall, squeezing to become invisible at the stage edge.

And then a clumsy move and a short sigh and Mrs. Wright's voice finding me like a siren: "Gail, dear? You still here?"

"Yes, Mrs. Wright."

A throaty cough preceded Mr. Hamilton's face, checking his watch as he emerged in the dimmed light. "Do you need a ride, Gail? Would you like me to call your mother?"

"Oh no. She's ... I'm ... She'll be here soon."

He nodded, put his hands in his pockets, rattled some change and turned back to Vera Wright. I stared again at the marching clock. 5:11.

Mr. Hamilton jangled his coins, I swung my legs, Mrs. Wright picked up her coat and then Mr Hamilton turned to leave.

"Well, good night then, Mrs. Wright." He strode out the door as he added, "See you tomorrow, Gail."

He couldn't have heard my quiet response over the loud echo of his heels on the linoleum. I looked at Mrs. Wright, standing now in front of the mirror as she put on her overcoat. She wrapped a silk scarf around her neck, tucking the ends beneath the coat's lapels, and then her shoulders slumped and her head bent forward. From behind I saw a spasm heave at her back as she fumbled at the wrist of each sleeve. I looked away in alarm as I heard her whimper, lifting a hanky to her eye.

Vera Wright, 1951 Arkansas Waltz Champion, would never break down in public. "If you're not feeling your best," she'd always said when one of us burst into tears over a nasty comment or a torn skirt, "go somewhere quiet and pull yourself together. Don't show your emotion to the men, dearies."

I concentrated on my feet, swinging them hard and letting the backs of my shoes bang against the stage wall, but stopping when I remembered that Mrs. Wright liked our shoes not to be scuffed.

Worried, I glanced over my shoulder and this time Mrs. Wright was reapplying her bright red lipstick. In the mirror her eyes met mine and she tried to smile back, but her eyes were watery and she pulled away from the mirror.

"Don't mind me, Gail, dearie. I'm a bit of a mess tonight."

A car horn sounded outside and I stood up quickly. I hesitated, seeing Mrs. Wright bent over her handkerchief again. Her skin was cold when I reached out to touch her wrist and my fingers left a pale, blotchy rose of colour.

"Mrs. Wright?"

She waved her hanky at me. "You go on home now, Gail. I'll be all right."

Our last meeting was a hot summer's afternoon when Peter and I were in the woods with another of his friends. I wore short shorts and a midi top, trying my best to be sexy, though still naïve about what made a sexual being. Peter and his friend had unearthed a stash of *Playboys* from a cache beneath a rock and the magazines, damp with mildew, lay open at several centrefolds.

"Look at the tits on Miss December!" Peter held his open hands in front of his chest, palms up.

His friend nodded in approval. "Hers that big?" he tilted his head at me.

I looked at Peter and saw him grinning in a way I didn't like. "Wanna see?" he asked his friend.

I shook my head at him. "Peter, don't be gross."

"C'mon—lemme show them off. He won't touch 'em or anything."

I struggled to get up from my cross-legged position and Peter grabbed for my wrist. The heat behind my eyes threatened to spill over as I yanked at my arm and pulled away.

"Hey, what's wrong with you?" He flung it at my back like a dirty word.

I ran, a slow fury of tears blurring everything with a sudden darkness. Thick ropes of salal grabbed at my ankles and I lifted my arms against the slap of overhead branches, unsure of the path. Dusk was still hours away and I couldn't understand when this sudden night had fallen, how the taunting woods had trapped me.

What He Wished For

Y ou know what Mom says?"
        The left side of Jake's mouth tightens but he doesn't take his
        eyes off the road.

"No," he says to Samantha, "but I bet you're going to tell me."

"She says you never take us anywhere nice on summer vacation because you're too cheap."

Jake stares at the vista of the BC interior beyond the windshield in front of him, rolling grassland yellowed by a long, dry summer and hills undulating into the distance, the cliché backdrop for a western. The Jack pines on the hillsides, sparse and scrawny, give meagre shade to clumps of white-faced cattle chewing mechanically and Jake wishes that he could transport himself, à la *Star Trek*, into the body of one of those brown beasts.

Jake nods his head in response, then says, "I guess she can think that about me if she likes." He's heard this complaint before, first from

85

Gloria and now from a daughter who seems to be following in her mother's footsteps.

Twelve-year-old Sam blows an oversized bubble with her chewing gum, letting it explode with gusto.

"Is that what you guys think?" Jake looks into the rear-view mirror, hoping to catch the eye of seven-year-old Jerry in the back seat. But Jerry is elsewhere, staring wide-eyed at the countryside beyond the car, completely removed from the conversation in the front. His one chance of support lost, Jake turns back to the road.

"She takes us to neat places," Samantha adds.

"You don't think it's neat hiking into the mountains, camping in an old gold miner's cabin and going to sleep listening to loons and coyotes?"

"I mean Disneyland."

"How many kids do you know who've been places like we have, huh?"

"You're just saying that because you don't like spending money."

Jake checks the person next to him, making sure it's his daughter and not his ex-wife leaning against the passenger door.

He takes a deep breath as he looks out his side window. "Look," he tries again. "It's okay for your mom to think I'm cheap, just like it's okay for me to think something else about her, but...."

"Don't say mean things about Mommy," Jerry's voice squeaks from behind.

"I'm not, Jer."

"But you're thinking them. I can hear your thoughts, Dad."

Jake finds his son in the rear-view mirror again. "You can?" he raises his eyebrows in mock disbelief. "I didn't know you were psychic!"

Jerry frowns briefly and then his face crumples. "I'm not!" he blubbers as the first salty splash runs down his cheek.

"Hey, Jer," Jake softens his voice. "What's up?"

"I'm not a psycho!"

"No, son!" Jake laughs. "Psychic doesn't mean—"

"Ha!" Samantha throws her head back against the headrest. "I told you you were weird!" she cackles.

"Am not!" Jerry howls.

"Are too!"

Jake feels his shoulder muscles tightening. After a month of summer vacation refereeing disagreements like this, the rushed and overtired weekends spent with them during the school year are beginning to seem more attractive. He'd naïvely envisioned a long period of reconnecting with the kids in a way that he realized wasn't going to happen and now Jake sags with the weight of being with them at all. He thinks how, if it were Gloria sitting there beside him and tossing insults and hurtful comments as though they were mere words, he'd stop the car, open the door and let her find her own way home.

"Sam—" he searches for a safe tone—"you wouldn't like it if Jerry said that about you."

"He says it all the time!" she spits. "He calls me names and if I get mad at him, he runs to Mom, the little baby!"

"Do not!"

"Do so! But now you're stuck with Dad. He's not gonna buy you off with ice cream or a new toy. Too bad, brat!"

Jake's foot hits the brake. He swerves onto the shoulder and slams the gearshift into PARK, then turns and takes Samantha's arm by the elbow, pinching it hard. "Why can't you learn when to stop, for Christ's sake! You're just like your mother!"

Sam's eyes widen with fear and then with venomous hate. She turns away from Jake, wrenching her arm from his hold. In the back seat, Jerry begins to wail. Jake twists uncomfortably, reaching a hand back to his son's knee. "It's okay, Jerry. I'm sorry."

Jerry rubs at his eyes with balled fists. Jake turns back and sees the way Sam has pressed herself against the passenger door panel. He reaches for her shoulder. "Sam—I shouldn't have said that. I'm sorry I lost it."

Sam lurches away from his hand.

Jake shuts his eyes and slumps in his seat, leaning his head against the headrest. He listens to his daughter's muted sobs beside him, her face squashed into the passenger window. From behind come his son's leaky snuffles.

Behind closed eyelids, Jake sucks a deep breath into his belly. He sighs it out long and slow through his open mouth, trying to focus on relaxing his neck and shoulders. He tries not to hear the thought in his head: No matter where we go, she's still there.

Jake looks across at the crumpled body of his daughter squeezed against the door. He decides to leave her alone for now and sits forward to put the car into gear, turn back onto the highway. He wants to take advantage of this silence in the car to regroup.

It is amazing, Jake thinks, how Sam can work him like a hawk, flushing him into the open and then diving for the kill as soon as his soft spots are exposed.

Gloria always said he was too sensitive. "It's not me leaning on all your buttons, honey," she used to say. "It's you not making your boundaries clear."

Gloria was ultra-clear about boundaries. Three years ago she'd asked Jake to change his and move out of the family home.

"I don't love you any more," she told him. "I've met someone else."

Jake had reacted in disbelief, pulling his wife against his chest and tucking her head beneath his chin where it had once nestled so snugly. But Gloria had pushed away and Jake had seen the way her eyes glistened, the same way they'd shone when Jake first met her.

The first time Merle came to the house, he was a dinner guest. Gloria sold life insurance and she liked to invite prospective clients into their home.

"I like them to see that I have a family, that I'm not doing this just for the money," she said. "That way they know I'm human too."

She and Jake had stood in the doorway and watched together as Merle parked his expensive motorcycle in their driveway. Jake saw someone in his late fifties climb off the bike, tucking a black helmet emblazoned with flying eagles under his arm as he strode up the path towards them.

The conversation had ended up around Merle's detailed knowledge of motorcycles, particularly the Honda Goldwing he rode.

"What a nerd," Jake said after he left.

"You think so?" Gloria seemed surprised.

"You don't?" Jake turned at the kitchen sink where he stood washing a wineglass, the bubbles of dish soap dripping onto the floor.

It was one of those telling moments that Jake went back to every time he fell into the trap of wondering where things had gone wrong, that memory of Gloria looking so surprised about Jake's opinion of Merle. Less than a year later, Gloria brought Merle home again, this time to stay.

Since Merle had moved in, Jake's status in the family home had slipped from all-important Father to Good Family Friend. As if to confirm the change, Gloria gave him a new title.

"Uncle Daddy's here," she called when Jake arrived for one of his first weekend visits with Sam and Jerry.

"Hey!" Jake bristled at her.

Gloria shrugged, avoiding his eyes. "They can't call both of you Dad."

Jake had wanted to make Gloria understand and so he grabbed the soft flesh of her upper arms in his long fingers. "Listen, Gloria," he hissed, shaking her to attention. "This time you've gone too far."

When she flung his hands off her arms, there were large red welts where he'd squeezed too hard.

Jake imagined Merle in his house—Jake's old house—tuning up the engines on the Honda Goldwing and Gloria's Saab, balancing the household accounts, cooking veal parmigiana for dinner, fixing all the broken things on the list Gloria kept taped on the fridge door, being the driven, ambitious person she had once sought in Jake.

It was hard not to want to blame everything on Merle. If the guy had shown any amount of sympathy when Jake came for the kids, maybe they could have worked things out. But after the arm-squeezing incident, Merle always came to the door with Gloria, his beefy body filling the entire gap beside hers. He stood there like some kind of sentinel while Jake waited for his kids to appear from somewhere behind their human fence.

When Jake picked Sam and Jerry up in early July, Gloria handed him a list of the kids' pre-set activities and summer lessons. "And don't forget to wash their clothes before bringing them home," she added.

Jake had clicked his heels together and saluted and Gloria had sneered, then shoved at the door. Before the slam, though, Jake saw the smirk on Merle's face. It was all he could do not to break down the door with his fists.

The intensity of his anger at Gloria unnerved Jake: he hadn't been this out of control while they were married. If Gloria had pissed him off in the old days with another of her unending requests, he had dealt with his annoyance by throwing himself into physical chores. He'd put the garbage into the battered aluminum cans then crash the lids on top as if they were cymbals, sometimes repeating the noise for effect. He tore at the starter cord of the lawnmower and drove the machine recklessly, maiming low-hanging branches on shrubs and bushes. And he ran the dog with such ferocity that even the long-legged mutt came home exhausted. Near the end, just before Gloria had told him she wanted out of the marriage, Jake made a final desperate attempt. He sent up prayers, silent prayers in the black of their bedroom, asking for a miracle to turn his life around, make this marriage bloom again. But Jake could feel their life together disappearing like water down the drain.

Sometimes when he feels the simmering low in his abdomen, that urgent roiling sensation that he feels now, Jake wonders how in hell Gloria and he had ever decided to marry, let alone have kids. Not that he wishes Sam and Jerry hadn't been born. He's never wished that, not even when he was packing to leave and hating Gloria with more fever than he'd ever felt in loving her.

It was the kids who made his life worth living and whose presence had sustained him through the worst of the separation. Now it was the memories of their early childhood and stories from special vacations like these that Jake clung to. He thought back to when Jerry had come home from the Sunday school classes Gloria had sent the kids to, the book he'd brought home when he was first learning to read. When Jake pulled his son onto his knee to listen to him read aloud, it was all he could do not to laugh when Jerry announced the title proudly: *Dog in Heaven*. Out of the corner of his eye, Jake had seen Gloria take Sam's hand and squeeze it, winking so that Sam wouldn't laugh at her brother's mistake. After that it had become a family saying: "That Big Dog in heaven isn't listening," they used to say whenever anything went wrong.

Jake takes his right hand off the steering wheel and massages the tightness at the back of his neck. For the briefest of moments, he allows himself to relax a vigilant hold on his feelings and to wish that just once the Big Dog would listen to him and take care of the Gloria problem.

On the stretch of road between Kamloops and Salmon Arm, a large green sign announces an upcoming exit: Highway 5A, an old road that winds through the cattle country south of Kamloops. Jake smiles, remembering childhood summers spent on a nearby ranch.

He breaks the silence in the car. "You guys want to see where real cowboys live?" He looks at Samantha, still twisted into the passenger door, only her back and shoulder presented to him, and then he peers into the mirror at his son.

Jerry sits up with interest. "Can we go riding?"

"Maybe. Want to try?"

"Sure!"

Jake reaches out a hand to Samantha but she curls away even tighter. Unwilling to give up, Jake strokes her slinky blonde hair. "Come on, Sammy—let's not have the last day of our holiday end in a fight."

He waits for a response from the other side of the car.

"Sam?"

When she speaks, the resentment is palpable. "I wish you were dead!"

As the car snakes along the old highway, Jake carries on a father-son banter with Jerry. He tries not to notice the hunched figure on his right whenever his eyes switch from the rear-view mirror to the road and he listens with escalating appreciation to Jerry's stupid, grade-school jokes.

"What's brown and sounds like a bell?" Jerry asks.

"I don't know."

"Dung!".

Jake slaps his thigh in approval. For a moment he wonders if Jerry's infatuation with bathroom humour shouldn't be outgrown by now and then he hoots with laughter.

An hour or so later Jake turns to see if Sam is coming out of her funk. Looking at the bony protuberance of her shoulder blades, he realizes that, in spite of all those years with Gloria, he's learned very little about love.

Highway 5A threads through miles of gentle hills into a twisting valley and as the road sinks into the earth, Jake feels as though he is slipping into his past. After half an hour they see a weather-beaten ranch off the side of the road. The spread is a poor one: the porch on the sagging house is at a dangerous incline and the roof of the old barn has gaping holes in it. But the silver in the aged siding of the buildings gives the farm a soft glow in the late summer sun.

"When I was little," Jake announces to Jerry and the still-withdrawn Samantha, "my dad brought me up here to work on my uncle's ranch. I used to spend whole summers here."

"What'd you do?" Jerry asks.

"Fed the animals, fixed fences. Helped my uncle wherever he needed it."

"Didja ride horses?"

"Every day."

"Can we go visit him?" Jerry leans over the front seat, hopeful.

"He's not here anymore, Jer. He died a long time ago."

"What happened to his farm?"

"I guess it got sold. Don't really know." Jake takes his foot off the gas pedal, slowing to take in the spread of grassland outside.

"Didn't he have a wife or a kid?"

"He had a wife, yeah. No kids."

"Didn't she stay on the farm?"

"No. She moved away afterwards."

"Why'd she do that?"

Jake shrugs. "Too hard, I guess. Too much for one person."

"Couldn't she find another husband?"

He smiles wistfully. "It's not as easy as that, Jerry." He puts his foot back on the gas and again the car picks up speed.

The heat of the afternoon sun beats through the passenger seat window and now, from beneath a restless sleep, Sam shifts in her seat. Jake turns at the sound of her movement and notices the sweat-dampened hair stuck to her forehead. He notices too that she's unfolded her tight body, relaxed the distance between them. He reaches for her hand and Sam's eyelids flutter at his touch but she doesn't wake. He glances in the rear-view mirror and sees Jerry, head lolling uncomfortably on his chest. He wonders about pulling over, stopping for a snooze himself.

The countryside mellows, sleepy creeks and more greenery breasting the road as it levels off. Jake remembers a myriad of lakes beyond sight of the highway and thinks that if he can recall which one is a good swimming hole, they should take advantage of this last afternoon together, drive home in the cool of the evening instead of this blazing heat. There isn't any need to rush, and anyway, Gloria is likely to be snappy at the sudden invasion of children into her quiet space.

The thought creates a vision of Gloria in a snit. The way her shoulders lift so high she looks like she's wearing football pads. The way her voice coughs out two- or three-word sentences, avoiding any prolongation of a conversation with him. The way her eyes seem permanently fused on an object behind Jake. As though looking into his eyes would crack her stony exterior.

Their last spat was over Merle. Jake had gone back to working the pipeline in northern Alberta, a job he'd had when first married. At Jerry's birth, though, Gloria insisted Jake find work closer to home. She pushed him to study for an MBA, and Jake entered the degree program as a part-time evening student. But when he realized the separation wasn't going to be a short haul, Jake used the situation as an excuse to drop his studies.

"I can't afford the fees if I'm paying child support, rent and part of the mortgage, Gloria," Jake said.

Gloria rolled her eyes and shook her head. "You don't want to succeed, do you, Jake?" she sighed at him.

So he'd gone back to the pipeline and spent those first few months watching the flares of the gas line shooting up to the heavens, hoping to learn something about paths of ascent. In that constant twilight beneath the northern summer stars, Jake ruminated about his failed marriage and what had gone wrong. Then one day he drove into the nearby town and called Gloria from a pay phone.

"Gloria," he said when she answered. "I understand now."

There was a tiny pause before she said, "I'm glad you've figured it out, Jake."

"I guess I needed to be alone, you know? To sit and think about it all."

"Sure."

"Look—I'm coming into town at the end of the month. How about we go out for dinner somewhere?"

"Jake, honey ..." Gloria's voice was low and sweet. Jake closed his eyes and listened to his heart thudding, the whoosh of big transports on the nearby highway. "I don't think that's a good idea," she breathed.

"Why not? Glo', listen—I'm going to call the lawyer. Tell him to put everything on hold. C'mon—let's at least talk."

"No, Jake."

"What's wrong?" Jake slumped against the glass door, his free hand on his brow.

"It's not going to work. It doesn't matter any more."

He stood in the phone booth looking out of town at the empty northern vista.

"Jake, I'm going to hang up now."

The dial tone stung his eardrum. Jake crashed down the receiver and then picked it up again and redialled. When Gloria's voice came on the answering machine, Jake screamed at her.

"Tell that prick to get the fuck out of my house!"

Sam stirs and Jake turns to look at her. He stretches out his arm and lays his hand on her shoulder, wondering what fields of thorns she'll make him cross in order to reach her after that last squabble.

"Dad?"

Jerry's small voice brings Jake's eyes to the mirror.

"You're back." He smiles at his son.

"I'm hungry."

"There's cheese and apples, some juice in the cooler."

"Can't we stop for a hamburger?"

"Not out here, buddy." Jake indicates the barrenness of the land beyond the car.

Jerry sits in a sleepy daze for a minute, yawning and staring out at the heat-miraged countryside.

"Want to stop for a swim?"

"Where?"

"Lots of lakes around."

Jerry looks out the other side of the car, frowns. "No, there aren't, Dad."

"Yep," Jake drawls, back in the saddle again. "Up there, behind the road." He points out the windshield, craning his neck to look as he does. "We can even go skinny dipping."

"Sam won't. She doesn't like people looking at her boops."

"Her what?"

"Boops."

"You mean her breasts?"

As if she's heard, Sam's eyelids lift, focusing on Jake's face with a stare of non-recognition.

"Hey, Beauty," Jake smiles at her.

"Yeah. Sam has breasts now," Jerry's voice continues in the back seat.

Sam's forehead buckles as she registers his voice. With a sudden twist she makes an animal lunge at her brother. "You little dink!" she spits.

Jake grabs her fist as she dives for Jerry.

"Sam," Jake keeps his voice soft. "He doesn't understand."

She clicks her tongue in the loudest demonstration of disgust she can make but withdraws her hand. Once again she crosses her arms and stares out the window to wish herself elsewhere.

Jake looks ahead, searching for landmarks. His breath is shallow, attentive to more signs of anger from the person beside him.

"Dad?" comes Jerry's querulous voice. "Can I sit in the front soon?"

At the side of his vision, Jake sees Sam's face twist into a mask of pure venom. And then outside the windshield he sees what he's been looking for.

An old willow stoops to brush its tendrils against the dusty earth of a rutted turn. "Here we are," Jake announces. "One of the best swimming holes in the world, coming right up!"

From where he sits on a towel near the shore, Jake watches Jerry, sees the layers of leftover baby fat folding over his shorts as the boy splashes in the lake, leaping and jumping as though the water were a trampoline. Sam, though, lingers at the edge, arms still crossed and toes barely touching the ripples at the shoreline. While she tests the water, Jake stands and rubs his hand over his thickening belly, stretching as he wades into the lake. He dives, then swims with long strokes, turning back near the other side of the small lake. Emerging from the water, Jake is panting as he reaches for a towel.

It occurs to Jake that if Sam has breasts, maybe she has also started menstruating. He turns as he towels his still-blond head of hair, tries to see through the arms she holds against her chest, wanting to hide what the bathing suit reveals. Jake senses a tightness in his throat as he recognizes that his daughter is leaving childhood. It makes him feel suddenly old, as though she has gone off on a world tour without saying goodbye. He understands that when she comes back, he may not recognize her any more; that she may not be the same person who left. Increasingly Jake feels like one of those fathers who doesn't know his child very well.

It was how he had felt during Sam's first visit to the orthodontist. After the specialist had introduced himself, he shut off the overhead lights and Jake was confronted by four lurid x-rays of Sam's skull hanging on the blue lightboard. And while the dentist pointed at irregularities and problems on the negatives, Jake found himself paralyzed by the dark holes of his daughter's eye sockets and the leer of her teeth on those shadowy transparencies. The vision choked at his heart and he felt himself withdraw from the dentist's presentation, reaching for Sam's hand in the chair beside his. But Sam, embarrassed or unwilling, pulled away from him, squirming to the far side of her chair, and Jake was left to face the absence of the soul in those blue outlines of bone and shadow.

"Hey, Dad!" Jake hears Jerry from somewhere outside his thoughts. "Can we fish in this lake?"

Jake turns his head to find his son but a sudden reflection off the water is so strong that he has to close his eyes, cover them with one palm. He reaches out his other hand, trying to balance himself from a reeling sensation, and waits for the instant of blindness to pass. He opens his eyes again and squints into the glare but can find only a black, shadowy shape somewhere across the water. He blinks as he attempts to walk, mesmerized by the sunspots in his vision and weaving like a drunk towards the lake.

"Dad?" Sam's voice reaches out from somewhere to the left of him. "Dad, are you okay?"

For the smallest instant Jake is disoriented enough to think the voice he hears is Gloria's, speaking with an old tenderness.

Jake stops, stares in the direction of the voice, squinting to see past the garish colours dancing in his vision. He shivers, reaches out a tentative hand. "I ... I think I got up too fast," he says, bending his neck and holding his face in his hands, willing the blood back to his brain.

The cool touch of a hand on his shoulder, another on his forearm. Sam.

Jake tries to joke himself back to the present. "For a minute there I thought we were all on the other side!"

"Why don't you come in the water with me and cool off, Dad." It's a demand, not an invitation, and Jake hears the fear in Sam's voice.

Hours later, back on the road headed south, Jake feels Sam's eyes sneaking sideways looks at him. He wonders if she's ready to talk about what happened earlier in the day. He is grateful—hungry—for her concern, feeling the huge gap of time since anyone has actively worried about him.

The sun is low in the sky and its rays pierce him from either side of the lowered visor. He drives with a hand held against the worst glare.

"Are you sure you're okay to drive, Dad?" Sam's voice is tentative, unsure.

"I'm fine, sweetie." Jake turns to her with an inquisitive brow. "Did you have a good afternoon?"

She doesn't look at him but she nods, even smiles a little. "The lake was beautiful, yeah."

Jake turns back to the road, pleased. "Want to go back some day?"

"Sure. But I was wondering...."

Jake glances at her. "What?"

"If you and Mom died, what would happen to us? To Jerry and me?"

Jake forces a weak laugh. "Why are you thinking about that, sweetie?"

Sam shrugs her bony shoulders against her still-wet hair and looks out the passenger window. "I just wanna know."

Jake glances at her again and shakes his head. "I guess you'd go live with Grandma and Grandpa."

"You aren't going to die, are you, Dad?" Jerry whines.

"Not me, Tiger. You guys got a lot more hiking and camping trips to do before I let you off the hook!"

Sam shakes her head. "I'm serious, Dad. And I don't want to live with Grandma and Grandpa."

Up ahead the highway disappears around a hairpin turn. SLOW TO 30 cautions the yellow road sign and Jake eases his foot onto the brake as the highway slips behind a rock face. He is speeding as he comes into the turn, doing closer to 45, but the car isn't straining and so halfway around the corner he releases the brake and reconnects with the gas pedal. He is coming out of the hairpin, increasing the speed, when he's forced to stomp on the brake. His right arm flies out to prevent Sam's skull from slamming into the dashboard as the car skids sideways and a huge semi-trailer, jacknifed across the double yellow line, looms into view. Against the streaming rays of the sunset, Jake sees the truck's emergency flashers dulled behind a cloud of dust still rising from the road.

"What's wrong?" Sam croaks when they stop.

"An accident." Jake puts the car in PARK as his eyes jump to the mirror. "You okay, Jer?"

Jerry's eyes are as large as saucers and Jake unfastens his seat belt to turn around. He reaches an arm out to both his kids.

Sam's fingers grab at his arm and Jake hears a tremor in her voice. "Someone's on the road."

Jake looks over his shoulder and sees the driver of the semi standing on the double line, removing his peaked cap and wiping his hand back from his brow, putting the cap back on and looking around, stunned.

"I'll go talk to him," Jake says, shutting off the engine. "You two okay?"

"No, Dad," Sam whimpers again. "Over there."

Jake swivels in his seat to look front again and now the full spectre of the scene comes into focus. Underneath the cab of the semi lie the crushed handlebars and front wheel of a motorcycle. Jagged pieces of chrome and metal are scattered between the shoulders of the highway like toys across a driveway. The truck driver lifts his head, sees Jake and begins walking towards the car.

His boots send feeble kicks at stray pieces of debris, as if to clear a path through the wreckage, and Jake sees him stoop to reach for something. Numbed by the vision of destruction, Jake wonders where the motorcyle driver is, realizing that he—or she—wouldn't have lived through the impact. He sees the trucker's boot jab at a round black object and then the driver stumbles, turns to retch.

A black helmet rocks in place where the driver's toe nudged it, a dark puddle of blood pooled underneath. The trucker finishes vomiting and turns back, giving the helmet a stronger shove to send it over the shoulder. The black roundness of the helmet wobbles, rolls half a turn and as it does, Jake sees the dead face.

"My God!" he whispers.

Sam whimpers as her fingers dig at him, her face burrowing into his shoulder.

"What's happened, Dad?" Jerry's hoarse whisper comes from behind.

Jake cradles his daughter's head, tucks it beneath his chin and notices the familiar way it feels nestling into him. He is aware of Sam's clinging hands and he feels the smallness of her body against his. He holds her trembling body close, unsure how to relieve her of the horror she has seen.

Jerry wiggles out of his seat belt, crouches between the bucket seats and presses himself against Jake's shoulder. Jake lifts an arm to pull his son in and all three of them huddle together until they hear the truck driver's tap at the window.

"You might wanna pull over." He points his chin at the shoulder. Jake nods and then they both stare at the litter of metal beside the car. "Maybe back aways," the trucker says.

As Jake puts the car in reverse, Sam makes room for Jerry in the front. When he puts his arm along the back of their seat, Jake sees the way Sam has wrapped her own arm around her brother, protecting him as much as herself, and he feels the beginning of a knot in his throat.

He backs up, easing onto the gravel shoulder as soon as a clear spot presents itself. He parks, then turns off the engine, starts to open the door before turning to the kids. "You guys okay?"

They nod at him and squeeze a little closer to each other, frozen in silence.

"I'll just be a minute." He gets out of the car, looks around to find the trucker behind him on the road, squatting in the middle of the curve to set a warning flare. Jake walks back and stands to one side, watching.

"You all right?" he asks when the trucker stands again. "You hurt at all?"

The older man shrugs and Jake sees his fingers fidgeting with a small, round item, turning it over and over like a lucky coin. "I couldn't do nothin',", the trucker shakes his head back and forth. He closes his fist around the object, then opens it again, stares at the piece of metal pressed into his palm.

Goldwing the round medallion says.

"They come round the corner in my lane." His hand trembles.

A shiver passes down Jake's neck and along his right shoulder and he lifts his hand to the spot.

When he feels his legs start to shake, Jake crouches down beside the trucker, drops his chin against his chest. He feels himself swallowed into the memory of dark sockets in his daughter's skull, the leering emptiness of that smile and the knowledge of its fragility. He thinks about Gloria waiting at home, wondering why they're late, and then he turns to look at the car, his car, wanting now to gather up his children and feel the pressure of their warm bodies against his chest.

The Other

You stand on the beach and feel the cold kiss of waves on your toes, the tug of water at your feet. There is something about being at land's edge, as though if you stepped off and into the water, into and under it, you might find something new, something better in the dark and the cold. But there is also that other something—intuition or gut feeling—that holds you back, prevents you from leaving all that's familiar in search of another, different life.

This is what you have learned about intuition: that it can be wrong. And even when it's right—when it comes from a place of logic—your heart can override it.

What you feel when he comes up behind you, this new man you've been spending a lot of time with, is not your normal reaction. He puts his hands on your shoulders and you wait, alert but not alarmed. And when he encircles you with his arms and lays his chin on your shoulder, you don't recognize the feeling that bubbles behind your solar plexus. You hesitate, surprised, and then you tip your head back, feel your smooth cheek against his rough one. And the bubbling increases, rippling through you like some kind of symptom and you wonder, for the shortest of moments, if this is what happiness feels like. But then you shiver, wondering where such an idea could have come from. You push it away, suppressing it for all you're worth and wishing that the prospect of sex didn't undermine your already limited common sense around men.

Your inclination is to run. It's the kind of irrational reaction you might feel on top of the Empire State Building. You know you can't fall off but when you walk to the edge of the observation deck, not too close, but close enough that when you stand on your toes and peer over to see how far down it is, the skin on the back of your thighs prickles and you hear that crazy voice that whispers, "Jump! Jump!" You know it's senseless, completely over the top, this reaction to being in the same room with such a different kind of man. But his goodness makes you want to back towards the door, open it noiselessly and slip out, tiptoe round the corner and break into full throttle.

The bubbling—or is it roiling?—in your gut makes it hard to concentrate, and you have to force yourself. So you turn your head, stare out the window and comment on the view of the sea, then move away from him, hoping distance will help. You sit on the couch and watch the waves, let yourself be caught up in their endless movement, synchronizing your breathing with the in-and-out of their procession. The pressure beneath your sternum diminishes with the hypnotic effect of the ocean and in this way you can stay in the room with this man, mesmerized by the soft blend of his voice with the water's.

Later you are full of fantasies. Fantasies that take over as soon as you leave his house and sit behind the wheel of your car, letting it drive while you indulge in thoughts of what happened back there next to the ocean. In the privacy of the night, you relive that moment of surprised pleasure with his lips soft on your collarbone, so natural that the movement from kitchen to bedroom fogged over the memory of the other—your #1—man. And afterwards, the rolling over in bed, the pure joy on discovering a curve of flesh beside you where before there was always an empty sheet after lovemaking. That presence alone made the new man's impotence seem such a small thing, surely just an anxiety over this first time together.

And when your fantasies refuse to dwindle, you allow yourself to project into an imagined future. Into coming in the door at night to the light of another human being. Into the idea that comfort might be a predictable existence at the end of a phone line. Into the possibility of something to hold onto when the rest of life descends with a vengeance.

You think you want it, so you let yourself dream. Imagining how it could be.

But the past refuses to be discarded. It gets in the way, clouding the image of this new man with the memory of the other, a man you've always thought of as your lover though he says he doesn't love you and insists it could never work between you. A man you call your #1 because of some regular sexual trysts during the past two years. A man who offers you nothing, really, but the opportunity to continue hoping.

You think of the time you've spent working up to the sparse place you have with #1. Now it is so easy to please and be pleased in bed and surely that's worth holding on to? Such a lot of work to throw away and have to start again, begin anew. And though you have him only sporadically—when he wants it and not always when you want it—you've learned to ignore the drawbacks and to tell yourself that infrequently is better than not at all. You use this rationale in spite of the regular warning signs from that part of you—the lower part, the part with the built-in thermostat and fluid production line—which says that time is running out; that when your body stops responding the way that #1 likes, he will leave for good and then you will have nothing. No love and no sex.

So you put a lot on this new man. You wonder if he can take you further than #1, beyond having to choose between sex or love. You give him a small test, telling him about the situation with #1, and he nods knowingly but says nothing, offers nothing.

And then you add, "I'm pretty messed up about him." Meaning, "I don't know if I should be here with you." Hoping he'll say, "It's okay. We'll work it out."

But what he says is, "It's okay. You'll work it out."

You continue to sleep with this new man anyway. You begin to think of him as #2, but only because you can't quite depose #1—not yet, though you are considering it—and you begin to compare them. You consider their bodies, their skills, their wealth and potential in all areas, and you decide that #2 is lesser in the first two categories, but greater in the latter two. #1, though more pleasing to the eye, is more of a challenge. More of what you've known before—mostly loss.

#2 is the unknown. When you stand at the shore and lift your eyes away from the waves at your feet, he is the horizon that seems so far away. Hard to believe that anything is different—better—over there. Yet he is gentler, kinder than men you've had before. He has a certain wariness about him that suggests he is shy but when you rant on the phone to him one evening, apologizing before you launch into it by letting him know that he's phoned at the wrong time (you've just had an argument with your son and you need to vent), he listens attentively. And then he responds with acceptance, a reaction that touches you so deeply you get off the phone quieted by your surprise.

The other man is more like you in ways you dislike about yourself: his crude single parenting is so familiar that it makes you squirm. He bawls at his kids in front of you whenever they annoy or frustrate him so that they, and you, are embarrassed by your presence. So that they, and you, have one more thing to surmount before you can ever be close.

The second man has never been married and never a parent, but he has nursed a demented father, moving back to the family home to care for this parent and then, two years in, making the decision to put him in care. Later, on daily visits to the hospital, he sat outside in his car, trying to muster the strength to go inside while crying his heart out for a father already lost so long ago. All this for a man who behaved viciously towards his daughter and ignored his son.

Vicious paternity is familiar to you. It is the only kind of fatherly love you have known and the kind for which—you can see by #2's eyes—he feels deep regret. For you, for all daughters, for the daughter he never had. So that when you talk about your own father, hiding your pain by choosing purposefully neutral diction, you can see his response is one of deep sorrow.

And when he meets your son, #2's presence softens the heart of that suspicious and doubting young man never before impressed by any of your male companions. In the company of this new man, your progeny opens like a vault and you watch, amazed at his warming to a complete stranger. It makes you feel, for the smallest instant, as though things could work out. Between you and him; between the two of them.

Your son is not like this with #1. Neither is #1 as open with him. When he phones, finds your son at home, he changes his mind about coming over.

"Not to be rude or anything, but I don't want to be there when he is." As if he can't stand him, or as if he knows your son won't stand for him either. They have met three, maybe four, times, but neither one will give the other a chance, will look at the possibility that it would make you happy to see them enjoy something—anything—about each other. Like oil and water, they're unmixable and permanently opposed.

And since you've done it before—tried to show your offspring the qualities of all those past hated men—you wonder if this time you should be listening to him. You try not to flinch when he says it out loud: "He's such a great guy." Speaking of #2. "Why don't you go out with him, Mom?"

Trying not to hear what he doesn't say: *Instead of that other creep.*

You say: "He has too many nervous tics." Trying to stop this discussion before it begins.

"Bet they'd go away with the right person."

He leans on those last three words, resurrecting a memory from the past. A dark afternoon, tea in a café where a strange-looking woman took you into a little back room and rolled her eyes as she went into a trance, telling you what you didn't want to hear. "You're going to meet someone—the right one—soon. The one to marry."

The ugly shiver you felt then returns. You don't want another marriage. You don't know if you want another lover. Sex, yes; but love as well? The image of #1 comes to mind and you feel suddenly empty.

And when you tell that to a new girlfriend, someone met through #2 and older than you—so even if you're old enough to know better but don't, maybe she does?—she nods with understanding. She knows about the #1 kind of man. She knows how easy it is to tell everyone else as well as yourself that things will change, he'll get better. He's just going through a hard time right now.

But then she grabs the handle of the invisible knife in your side and gives it a sharp twist: "Isn't it sad that we can have sex with a guy but the idea of real intimacy scares the hell out of us?" She turns to look very pointedly at you, this friend of #2, so that you have to glance away when she says, "You know he's very taken by you?"

"He drinks too much."

"He's trying to change. He's a good person."

"I know." But you don't want to.

"He's just as scared as you."

You get up and move away from her, walk further along the beach beside the waves. You look at them coming at you and you imagine them washing over you. You think about how it would be to walk into them, feel them surround you, pull you under. With love.

But you don't know how that feels. You've never known the tug of love and maybe this isn't it either. Maybe it's only another lure. Maybe that unrecognizable bubbling in your gut is some kind of trick. Or maybe not.

You turn back in your mind, searching for a memory to hold on to and it comes as the rough touch of #1's palm on your skin, the way his bulging man's body covers yours in the act. You think about the way this new man can't quite compare to the good hardness of your #1 and you worry that #2 may have a long-term—rest of his life—problem with impotency. You acknowledge the fact that #2 is a safe harbour and that the other is—at best—a stormy ride. A ride full of nausea and staring out to sea and wondering why you're there. And for another brief moment you consider whether you missed out on one of life's basic lessons: the lesson about how to differentiate between what is real—what is important—and what is not.

You stand in the cold water and feel your toes begin to freeze and it is not unlike being on the verge of sex: common sense tells you not to go there but hunger pulls you under. You respond to a watery memory of #1 and you feel yourself buckling. You understand, as your consciousness slips away, that there is something much stronger than intelligence working at you.

You remember that first impulse to turn and run from #2 and you wonder if it was some kind of sign, the mind searching records of past experience.

You ignore the thought that you've never had much common sense around men, that love and desire seem somehow the same.

The disconnect of heart and head.

Threshold

"Why do you need a door there?" Mick frowns at Bea. She turns away with a roll of her eyes, so he backpedals quickly. "You already got a door on this side of the house."

"But it's not where I want it. And besides, it's warped and barely opens and closes."

Mick notices her suddenly crossed arms and flexing jaw muscles, her eyes dark with determination. Stubborn, he thinks. And then he understands what he likes about this woman: she knows exactly what she wants, is definite about it.

"Okay." He grins to lighten the tone. "Just please don't say later that you made a mistake?"

"Trust me." She shakes her head. But she still looks peeved at him for doubting her.

As he gets ready to cut into the kitchen wall, Mick can hear Bea in the next room, tapping away at her computer keyboard. He smiles at the noise, thinks how much it sounds like the chatter of a squirrel.

He holds up his carpenter's square and marks an X on the wall in front of him, imitating the sound of a squirrel's call as he does. It's a noise he likes to tease his dog with. "Where is it, Tracker?" He'll point at a tree. "Go find that squirrel! Go get him!"

Mick glances over his shoulder now, wondering if Bea heard him. Despite the fact that six weeks ago they'd gone past the boundary dividing friendship from the regions beyond, he feels somewhat restrained around her. She seems a little too classy for him, always dressed up and using words he doesn't recognize. Mick wonders if that's why he's been holding back from opening fully to her.

Still, in the short time they've come to know each other, the connection with Bea has taken on a surprising importance. This renovation she wants is a case in point: when Mick arrived early in the morning, he made that second, weak, attempt to talk her out of the new doorway, scared that she, like some other women, would change her mind after he'd already cut a hole in the wall. Now he stands back from the markings he's made there and shakes his head again.

"What's the worst that can happen?" he asks himself. And he knows the answer is what he doesn't want—that in the middle of the job she'll tell him to close it up, and he will feel cheated somehow; as if he'd wasted his time and couldn't even charge her for the job.

But it's not the money. Mick doesn't levy a full accounting when a customer is unhappy, and this time there is something much deeper pulling at him; something Mick can't quite put his finger on.

He pauses as sensual memories from last night's lovemaking overtake him. He wonders if Bea hasn't enchanted him, cast some sort of spell. It isn't only the way her image leaps regularly to mind, but the way he'll suddenly catch a whiff of her scent or a memory of her touch throughout his day. He'll be planing a board or sanding a windowsill and he'll see the way she looked at him as he made love to her the night before and then the sickening yearning that is still so new will rise in his gut.

Mick likes the whole package, the mix of intelligence, gentleness and sexual energy that Bea carries around. Even if he couldn't go all the way—live with or marry her—he'd like to maintain a friendship. More would be better, but at least working on her house gives him the chance to spend time with her; the possibility of developing more than their sexual compatibility.

He reaches for his work belt, buckling it across his hips and replaying her mysterious comment from last night.

"He's not a lover, really," Bea had said of another man in her life. Mick had felt a sudden tension at the possibility that he might be wasting his time, but he wanted to believe her so he let the words dissolve in the air. Still, he's treading with caution ever since that disclosure. He's carrying the information like an expensive new tool, handling it with care while learning about it.

He thinks about the other guy, wonders who he is and just where he fits into Bea's life. Mick senses that she isn't telling him everything, and the idea that she is seeing both of them, maybe sleeping with both of them, leaves him slightly nauseous.

"We're two peas in a pod," he'd said to her one night between periods of a hockey game. She responded with a goofy smile and he pulled her head against his chest, gave her a noogie. Bea's intensity was a thrill—the way she held his eyes when he looked at her, the way she rose to meet him in bed—and Mick sensed she wanted what he wanted. But she laughed when he pointed that out to her.

"What do you want, then?" she teased.

"A life partner. A best buddy and a mate."

And he'd known, by the way she said nothing, only lifted his arm off her shoulder and got up to make tea, that he was right. They were well matched.

Ever since then, Mick has been playing games with himself. Doing laundry one Saturday, he notices the box of soap getting low and he makes a prediction: *By the time this is empty, we'll have spent a whole night together.*

Another day, digging in the garden, he unearths an old kitchen fork. He picks it up and hefts it, then looks over at the garden shed forty feet away. He runs his thumb over the dull tines and positions the handle against his palm, readying it to throw. *If it sticks, it'll be more than an affair.* And when the fork circles through the air and lands with a *thwup* in the cedar siding, Mick holds his breath, waiting to see if it will fall out. The handle wobbles a minute, then stills, the tines embedded in the wall, true.

So was it just a fluke when, that first night Bea stayed with him, the next day he ran out of laundry soap? And was it mere coincidence when, the week he threw the rusty old fork at the garden shed, she came for dinner and afterwards, as they did the dishes, she put her soapy arms around his neck and whispered, "You're my guy," in his ear?

Maybe he's being soppy, reading simple signs as proof of what he'd like, but Mick wants to believe otherwise. The next time it happens, he's convinced that fate is at work.

On a Friday at the end of a long week full of problem jobs, Mick is on a steep roof finishing a chimney installation. Black clouds have been moving across the sky all day, threatening to rain and cancel completion of the tricky job, but so far he's been lucky. Attaching the collar of the pipe insert, he comes to the last slot and digs in his work belt for one more sheet metal screw. He pulls out handfuls of sawdust mixed with nails and rivets, but no screws.

"Aw, come on," he moans to himself. "One lousy screw." It's a long way down the ladder for such a small thing and he tries again, sifting through another handful of sawdust. When the fitting eludes him still, Mick curses in disgust and stands to go to the ladder.

As he swings his foot over the top bar, a picture of Bea appears in his head, her mouth open in laughter. Seeing her happiness right in front of him, Mick grins. He hesitates, then removes his foot from the top rung and shoves his hand back into the work belt, bringing out another fist of sawdust. This time, butting out of the shavings in his calloused palm, he sees the round head of a solitary metal screw.

Mick closes his fist and turns back to the chimney. He kneels to fit the screw into the final slot and aims the drill at it. The drill whines, then slows to a groan, and Mick smoothes his hand over the collar's edge to check that it's flush. He sits back on his heels, looking around at the finished job and whistling in satisfaction. "Gonna work this thing out," he says. His head nods a while, backing up the statement.

Mick's fear, standing in front of the markings for Bea's new door, is one of opening up the wall and finding the proverbial can of worms: wiring that has to be moved or dry rot that needs replacing before he can begin the framing. If that happens, he'll be here for a week instead of the two days he's allotted. Not that he doesn't want to be here, but he's worried this obsession over Bea is messing with his head.

The phone rings and Mick hears her answer it. He shoves the battery pack in his drill and aims the large bit at the corner markings. When he presses the power button, the noise drowns out her voice.

Five years earlier Mick had installed a wood stove here. At the time, Bea had just moved in and the living room was strewn with half-unpacked boxes. Mick had struggled to find a clear spot to put down the heavy cast-iron stove and unwieldy pipes for the job. While she sorted her stuff, Bea asked lots of questions about hiking in the local mountains. Mick had told her, his head up the chimney half the time, about his trips into the Caren range, the nearby wilderness area still unspoiled by logging or mining. On a whim he'd asked if she'd like to go with him next time he went up the mountain, and when he left the job site that day, he'd gone with a light skip in his step.

But the hike never happened. Mick had a change of heart about his invitation and didn't feel able to explain to Bea. Though he carried her image in his head for weeks, he told himself she was just someone met through work, nobody special. But he couldn't prevent the thoughts of her that rose throughout the day, and so the inevitable comparison between Bea and his girlfriend-of-the-time became a constant jab in his ribs. Things with Ros had been breaking down for a while, and the notion that Bea might be able to turn his life around made Mick feel wistful and not a little guilty. The guilt finally rode him and he began to try a little harder to rescue the sinking ship at home.

"No going back now, I guess." Mick hears Bea's voice when the drill shuts down.

He turns to see her standing in the office doorway. The lighting behind emphasizes her dark silhouette.

"Nope," he says. "Not unless you want a helluva big window instead?"

She smiles at his weak attempt at humour and turns away. Once again Mick feels a strange tightening in his chest, the feeling that has been lodged there for the past few months of getting to know her. He shivers and turns to put down the drill, find his chisel.

After Ros, Mick had tried to quell his desires. No more, he'd told himself after their breakup; no more women who can't commit to going all the way, to working it out and making it stick.

He places the chisel's tip against the drilled hole and slams the hammer against it, the memory of his former partner still rankling. It pissed him off how he'd put so much into their life together and then she'd dumped him as though nothing he'd done had meant anything or touched her heart at all. "I don't think I ever really loved you," she'd said. "I don't think I know what love is."

And here he was again, falling for another one who might—how could he know for sure?—be using him.

He steps back from the wall, ducks his head around her office doorway. "Bea? I'm gonna start up the chainsaw now. You ready?"

She is standing at the filing cabinet with her back to him. "Okay. Thanks," she says. Her voice is soft, barely audible, a trait Mick has noticed before and which has made him wonder if he's going deaf. But Bea has told him that she is sensitive to noise; that she loves quiet. He tries not to think about how she'd react to being around power tools all day.

Outside the house he fires up the saw, revving the motor to discourage its tendency to stall. Like so many of his tools, the damned thing needed maintenance but he'd been spending too much time with Bea to keep up with smaller chores. He smiles at that. He'd choose the chaos of disorganization any day if it meant more joy in his life.

He puts on his safety goggles and stands spread-eagled, aiming the heavy blade at the siding in front of him. But as the first whine rips into the cedar, he feels another pang of regret for allowing Bea to talk him into this job.

After minutes of the blazing noise, Mick puts down the sputtering saw and rips out a remaining chunk of siding with his hands. He peers into the opening made in the outside wall and nods in approval. No wiring to reroute, no 2x4s to move. He picks up the chainsaw and revs it again. Manipulating the tip of the chain with the delicacy of a fine carving tool, he rips a small tear in the drywall, then shuts off the saw completely.

Inside the house he uses the reciprocating saw to cut, then remove, several chunks from the other side of the wall. He finds himself smiling, then he laughs out loud, a whoop of pleasure.

"What?" says Bea from the office doorway.

He holds out a large work-calloused hand to show her the hole he's made. "Look at that!" he beams. "Piece of cake!"

Bea walks toward him with eyebrows raised. Mick watches the sway of her hips before turning hurriedly away. He wants to pick her up, swing her around for joy, but it feels too soon to be that easy with her. Naked in his arms she is passionate, but dressed she seems businesslike and distant. Such a thin threshold.

"It's almost like somebody had planned a door here," he says, leaning into the gaping wall. "Look at it—the framing's already in place." Mick steps through the opening and struggles to lift the new door in its frame, grunting as he slides it into temporary position. "Fits like a glove, eh?" He turns to show her his pleasure and finds her staring. But it's at him, not at the doorway, and there's another look—a glint of mischief—in her eyes.

"So maybe there was a door there before and a man decided to close it off for some dumb male reason. Maybe the little woman left him and he was so pissed with her that he up and shut the opening, d'ya think?"

For a moment Mick wonders whether she is laughing at his simpleness, his joy with a situation as banal as this door frame. He knows he is way beyond his usual ken with this woman; beside her he is nothing but a bush-league redneck. But still he feels it, that strange insistence of connection, as though some invisible force is pushing them together.

"It's just that—" he begins. "Aw, you don't know how often it happens that I do a favour for a friend—for free or for cost or whatever— and I get in there and it's a huge mistake, you know?"

She shakes her head at him, frowning. "This isn't a favour, Mick. It's a job."

Mick looks at Bea's worried expression and tips his head. "You don't understand," he tries. "I *want* to do this for you." And before he thinks about what he's doing, he reaches out to her, cups her small chin in his big hand.

Bea doesn't back away, only lifts her eyes. And he sees how she looks straight at him, how she lets his eyes mine her depths, as if she is not afraid of where this could go, this anticipation between them. Mick feels himself sinking a little further into her world and he wonders if he should say something, tell her how he's feeling.

But she turns away as quickly as she had opened up, and he is suddenly embarrassed for having wanted to read more into in her simple gesture.

"Would you like a sandwich?" she offers, moving towards the kitchen.

"Love one," he answers and turns back to the doorway. He shoulders the door frame, loosening it again as she opens the fridge. And as they work side by side, he can feel her intermittent gaze on his back.

"I like this," she says after a few minutes of listening to the pounding hammer breaking their silence. "It's like playing house with you."

Mick grins at the doorway in front of him. He wants to kiss her for saying that; lean in and hold her close, feel her body next to his again. He wants to ask about that other man too, whether Bea is ready to let him go or not. He stands in front of the new opening, waiting for the words to come.

"Here." Bea puts his sandwich on the table across from the empty doorway. "You can look at your work while you munch."

Mick's shoulders drop and he breathes out. He nods, then bends to put down the hammer and unbuckle his belt, dropping it on the floor.

But it is Bea who stares at the doorway as they eat, asking questions that Mick wouldn't have expected of a woman who's a financial advisor.

"So do you have to adjust the threshold at the bottom or do you adjust the framing at the top instead?"

And he tells her, again, how perfect the opening is; how very little adjusting is needed at all, if any. "It's as though this was waiting for me to come along and do the job, you know?" He shakes his head in wonderment.

Bea's eyes twinkle when she turns to smile at him. "Like us, Mick?" Her eyebrows and forehead lift in a question. "Are we the perfect fit too?"

Mick's lips twist in an effort at a smile but he swings his eyes away from hers and concentrates on the doorway. Not if there's three of us involved, he thinks.

"Better get back to it," he mutters, standing to put his plate in the kitchen sink. And as he bends for his work belt, he feels a strange softness in his knees, as though the ground beneath his feet is sinking.

At home later, Mick replays Bea's question while hefting boulders into place for a stone wall. He struggles to lift the big stones and as he manoeuvres each one, he feels the strain of his abdominal muscles. He recalls Bea's soft touch across his rippled belly, the way she stroked the hair there. The strong tactile memory arouses him so that he has to stop, put down the weight in his arms and rest a minute. But when he lets go, the boulder teeters and rolls off the top layer, dropping onto the ground and rolling across his toe. Mick swears and shoves at the rock.

He sits on the foundation layer, wipes at his brow and spits. Reaching for some water, he drinks long and hard from the bottle, then leans back, lifts his sore foot and wiggles his toes in the workboot. He stands again, tests his weight on the foot and grunts in satisfaction.

When he removes his boot later, Mick sees that the big toe of his right foot has developed a dark bruise under the nail. The thin, black scar sits like a portentous shadow and Mick wonders whether it's toxic, if some sliver of cedar or metal is the real cause of the pooled blood. The rest of the nail is intact, unbruised and unblemished. Mick scrutinizes the blackness and makes another prophesy: *When it's grown out, this thing with Bea will be settled.*

Bea goes away on a business trip and it is several weeks before Mick hears from her. She leaves a message on his answering machine.

"Hey, Mick—just to say I'm really happy to have the new door where I always wanted one."

But she doesn't suggest they get together for a walk or dinner and Mick knows that the other man is still in the picture. For another week he fights the desire to see her and then he gives in, stops by on his way home one night when he sees her car.

"Look, I'm having a hard time with this," he blurts out when she gives him a hug. "I just want to tell you how good this could be, you and me, you know?" In the opening that follows, Mick feels the futility of his words and wishes he could take them back.

But Bea doesn't turn away. Instead she nods understandingly and her eyes move from one to the other of his. After a long pause she puts her hands on top of his shoulders. "So maybe I shouldn't be asking if you can do another job for me, Mick?"

Mick grits his teeth, wondering if he can hang on long enough to wait for her answer.

"The old door," says Bea when he doesn't respond. She drops her hands and tilts her head towards the back of the house. "What do you think about putting a tall, narrow window there instead?"

Mick nods at the floor. "Yeah?"

Bea slides her hand into his and tugs him with her. "Glass blocks maybe? Lighten it up in here."

"Sure," says Mick. He concentrates on his breathing, the touch of her hand.

"Would it take long?"

"Day or two, maybe." He shrugs.

"Are you busy right now? Can you do it soon?"

Mick shakes his head, mute.

"Does that mean 'no, you're not busy' or 'no, you can't do it'?"

"Next couple of weeks?"

Mick builds the glass-block window for Bea and once again he is struck by the perfection of the set-up. The framing for the narrow old door accommodates a triple row of blocks without having to adjust the width. He frames in the bottom of the old doorway and creates a sill for the new window.

"It's like you," Bea says when she sees Mick kneeling at the sill opening. He raises his eyebrows and she laughs her soft laugh. "Long and skinny."

A hot rush of blood like a roar of water through the floodgate fills his guts. He remembers the black strip of bruise under his toenail, how in the bath last night he'd noticed it was almost grown out. The prediction that this thing with Bea would be decided by now had come back to him, and he'd wondered again if he was trying too hard to force an impossible situation. He'd found the nail clippers to trim the nail but something had stopped him. Still too soon.

The old door sealed off, the new window installed, Mick's contact with Bea pulls back once more. During long nights at home, Mick waits for her call, wondering if she will or if it was all in his head, whether he should call her. It is almost two weeks later, lying in the dark of his bedroom one night, when Tracker's bark alerts him to the sound of tires on the gravel drive. He sits up, stands to go to the front door. Peering into the night shadows, he waits for his eyes to adjust, and after a moment a moving silhouette sets off the motion detector lights.

Her figure moves in silence across the lawn and Tracker sits up in recognition.

"Hey, boy!" Bea bends to pat the dog when he rushes her.

"He figured you for a bear," Mick says from the doorway. "Didn't you hear him barking?"

"Sorry—I guess I should have warned you." Bea hesitates but Mick doesn't move, both hands holding either side of the door frame.

"I brought you a cheque." She steps forward, holding it out to him.

Mick tilts his head quizzically, crossing his arms and letting his tall figure block the threshold. He takes a breath and starts to speak. "Why didn't you phone and—"

Bea lifts her hand, puts a finger to his lips.

"It's done now," she murmurs. She plumbs his shadowed eyes, then drops her hand to tug at the knot of his arms. Tucking the cheque into one of his freed hands, she wraps the other around her neck and pulls him into a hug.

"What about him?" Mick asks from above her head. "Is he done too?"

From the place where her cheek rests on his chest, Bea's voice is muffled. "It's cold, Mick. Let's go inside."

Syncopation

B eside the phone is an old photo of Amy at three years of age. It shows a young child in profile, the white handset almost as big as her small head, a red plastic barrette clipped to the side of her blonde hair. Arlene took the photo on one of the first occasions that her daughter answered the phone, when the machine was still a mystery to the child. In the photo Amy's lips are slightly parted as she listens, intent on the voice at the other end of the line. She has not yet understood how it is that she can hear the words of a person who is so distant.

The telephone rings and Arlene lifts the receiver to her ear, frowning at the static on the line. The phone has been dropped by her or by Amy so many times that it works only sporadically. She jiggles the cord, trying to fix it in a certain position, make the crackling disappear.

"Hello?" she asks when the noise stops.

"Happy birthday," says Geoff's disembodied voice.

Last she'd heard, Geoff was on the other side of the country. She wonders why he's calling now; knows well enough that her birthday is just an excuse.

"Well, thank you," she says anyway. She feels a prickle of anticipation, an old sensation like the beginnings of a rising fever.

It's what she used to feel when the two of them walked onto a dance floor, a current running between them as they moved from the shadows onto the light-spattered hardwood. Loud music racing in her veins, muscles responding with small, uncontrolled jerks until she found the rhythm with him.

Here—now—Arlene can't tell if her anticipation comes from gladness or from vanity. She wishes she could say it was only from gladness.

She waits for his invitation: "Do you want to dance?" When nothing happens, she hesitates in the small silence of emptiness at his end of the phone line.

But she doesn't want to sidestep him like she used to and she says, "I heard through the grapevine that you would never talk to me again so I assumed there was no point in calling you."

"Yeah, well," he mutters.

Those murky shadows beyond the strobe-lit floors, the way the first strains of a familiar song nudged at them, their boiling urgency. Now it's there again, that feeling of wanting to explode beyond the self. And the feeling of needing to stifle it.

"Look, Arlene," he begins. "I still have very strong feelings so I guess it really depends on what day you get me." She closes her eyes, remembers his hand on the small of her back, how he was such a strong lead.

"I understand that, Geoff," she says, and she does. "But I think it's sad we can't be friends after all we've been through."

"There's still a lot of ugly stuff around your decision to leave," he barks.

She pushes away a hot instinct to return the blame, fumbles to stay in step.

"How are you?" she asks. She has forgotten, until it's out there, what he always answers to that question. For a split second she hopes he will stay inside the box, skirt the truth.

"Terrible."

Stupid of her. "Are you in Montreal?"

"Yes."

"I thought you liked it there. I thought that's where you wanted to be."

"I did."

Another lull before she says, "You're not making friends, then?"

"Yeah, but it's not the same as having the friends you've known all your life."

During one of their last quarrels, Geoff had called his friends a bunch of hypocritical no-minds, stuck in their ways and not going anywhere, and Arlene had asked why he maintained anything with them if he felt that way. He told her then it was none of her affair and who was she to talk anyway, having only one, maybe two, friends in the whole world.

Before all that, though, they'd been like fine-tuned musicians wedded to their instruments, spinning and stepping beneath the lights. They'd made such pretty harmony together, hot and steamy and nowhere near the real world. When they danced, it was obvious they belonged together.

Arlene thinks they must have outgrown the basic steps, wanting to discover something more in each other. Which was how they'd ended up walking along the river dike on a grey November day, a day so cold that after an hour she wanted to go home. But Geoff urged her on.

"Let's go a little further. Sit on that log over there."

A few minutes later he slid off the log and knelt in the sand, as if to get out of the wind. He fumbled in his pocket and pulled out some foil-wrapped chocolate in the shape of a bear. "For you," he said.

She leaned over and kissed his forehead, putting the bear into her own pocket for later. "Thanks, sweetie!"

"No, eat it now!" He was so insistent that she bit off the bear's ears, then offered it to him. He nibbled at the paws and gave it back, watching as she chewed the head off. The bear was hollow; a piece of paper nestled inside.

The words were written in careful calligraphy. "I couldn't bear it if you said no...." She read them, then looked at his deep brown eyes with her own blank ones.

"No to what?" she asked, feeling the hairs on her neck lift as she spoke. Her nose began to run and she sniffed loudly, wanting to get out of the cold quickly now. But he stayed on his knees, took her hand in his.

"Will you marry me?"

She could tell, when she replayed the scene later in her memory, how carefully he'd planned the whole thing. She knew that she should have been touched but what she really felt was embarrassed. For Geoff and all his fantasies about the way things should be done.

She'd hoped that marriage would be a continuation of those close nights on the dance floors, his hand pressed against the heat of her skin, her ribs rising to the light brush of his fingers.

Pure synchronicity.

As if nothing has changed, Arlene feels herself bending again with Geoff's dips. "But you still like the job?" she persists. "And I heard they're paying for your courses—that's good, isn't it?"

"Yeah, but having worked in the field for eighteen years, listening to professors tell me how it is doesn't cut it, you know? I mean, it's really a lot of bullshit, just a paper chase. And they're only giving me transfer credit for one year."

"That's all you were going to get here."

"No, they said two years."

"No," she argues with conviction. "I remember it was only one." In the pause she sees his pout—the furrowed brow and sulky mouth—and she softens. "Or maybe one and a half, was it?"

"Whatever. It's the shits."

The same old lead.

They'd been so good together. Better than good. All those many perspiring nights spent on polished floors, marking time with their arms and legs. As if by turning faster and faster they could make the problems disappear.

Now Arlene wants to slow it down. "Does this phone call mean it's okay to write?" she asks.

He waits a moment and she wonders if he is thinking about whether he wants her to write or about the letters she and Amy have already sent him. Letters he never answered; letters he told a mutual friend were mere tokens. Tokens of what? she had wondered. Affection? Isn't it okay to have affection for someone once loved?

She'd made him wait for her answer. Not so she could think about it, but because his proposal made her numb. For a whole afternoon and night he followed her from room to room, quietly, carefully, waiting for her response. In the end she couldn't stand to see him so desperate and she said yes.

What she'd thought was, Geoff wants a partner; Amy needs a father.

But she felt like Atlas, the weight of the world on her shoulders, staggering between heaven and hell.

His silence this time is so long that Arlene finds herself listening to the music behind him.

"I guess you can write if you want," Geoff says finally. She concentrates on the song instead of the coldness in his answer. She is surprised to hear, in the swell and fade of guitar riffs, a distinct twang.

"Are you still at the same address?" she asks before he can add the *but*.

"No. I've moved." He hesitates. "You could send it to the office and I'll get it there."

She remembers how he loved to talk about himself, and the memory makes her wonder about his request. Would getting a letter from a woman at his place of work impress his co-workers? Would he let them know it was from his ex-wife, suggest that she wanted him back? Or tell them what a nag she had been, always on his case about being such a slob around the house?

Or maybe there's someone he'd like to make jealous. Maybe that's what this out-of-the-blue phone call is about. Maybe there's someone who has him thinking about his past love affairs, particularly the big one—the marriage—and he's scared. Scared it could all happen again. The dance of love.

One night Arlene had gone dancing without Geoff. She went to a bachelorette party at a country and western bar and came home late and sloppy with too much drink. But she had wanted to teach him the two-step learned from the leather- and bourbon-smelling men at the tavern, so she placed his hands on the bony curve of her hips, pulling his own flat pelvis towards her and pressing up against him. She lifted her bloodshot eyes to his, giggling as she tried to demonstrate the syncopated movement of the feet, but after two failed attempts, Geoff pulled away.

"Is this what you did all night—rubbed up against hicks?"

"No, sweetie. C'mon—I'll try again."

"I don't want to learn a bloody cowboy dance! I don't even like that excuse for music!"

He'd stomped away in a tantrum of childish proportion and Arlene had felt sorry for herself at the time. But when Amy came into the living room a few minutes later, wakened by Geoff's loud voice, Arlene took the small body in her arms and began to twirl around with her daughter instead of her husband. In the middle of the dance she heard a door slam down the hall.

Now she feels sorry for Geoff. Sorry that he cannot move beyond the hurt he clings to; sorry that he won't get on with his life. She thinks how maybe she should've ended their dance after that failed two-step.

"But don't forget," Geoff's voice calls to her again. "You probably won't get a letter back."

"Okay," she answers. And as soon she says it, she knows it's not okay. Why does she still let him lead? Is she trying to resurrect a partnership? Or does she just want one last dance? She leans against the wall, sits this one out.

But she can't help remembering how they used to stand on the edge of the floor between sets, feeling the crazy race of their heartbeats, the dampness on their skin. The distance between them even then.

In the wake of the next silence, Arlene feels the way her pulse idles gently beneath her skin, dry and cold. She feels the space between them, feels herself stepping away from Geoff, the way she did in their last year together. It was the only way she could stay with him then, to have her mind somewhere else.

Sometimes Geoff could be persuaded to skip the dancing and then they'd go out as a threesome, taking Amy to the movies or a baseball game. But it seemed to Arlene that Geoff's personality changed then. He became harsh and more authoritative, as if he saw himself as a figurehead, the epitome of Father. He checked Amy's behaviour constantly, demanding an unrealistic maturity as though her childishness might somehow reflect on him.

"It's okay," she'd whisper to Amy when the child was upset. "Dad's tired today."

And later she'd hiss at Geoff, "Don't be so hard on her. She's just a kid."

The day they took Amy to see *Bambi*, the five-year-old burst into loud wails when the young stag was felled by a hunter. Without hesitation, Geoff leaned across Arlene in the dark theatre and slapped the child's leg. "Stop being such a silly little girl!" he hissed.

Arlene held the small body on her lap the whole way home, listening to the threatening silence in the car.

Everything coming apart.

That night she sat awake in the dark living room, listening to music, unable to sleep beside the warm body of such a cold man.

A nasal singer croons in her ear and Arlene strains to hear it. An electric fiddle winds into the melody. Country and western music at Geoff's house. Is he trying to let her know he's changed partners or just make a point?

"*So darlin' don't forget me* ...." Arlene tries to focus on the vocalist but Geoff's tone pulls her back.

"...I really don't know why you married me in the first place, Arlene," she hears him say and she nods in agreement.

He is talking about everything that went wrong again, going over all the details like a broken recording. "... and the way you played me afterwards. What was that all about, anyway?"

The quickening tempo.

At first she held on to the special memories: skating at midnight, the rink quiet after the Zamboni slid through the hole in the boards, the peculiar smell of ozone tickling her nostrils. Walking through the snow to get a video on a sub-zero night and falling asleep on Geoff's chest while he watched a ridiculous horror film. Hiking the West Coast Trail in a summer storm. Moving together across the light-spattered floor, the sweaty release after the closeness, like the release after sex.

But slowly, like a tango, their dance had grown into a rage. Arlene began to balk at her husband's childish ways, his ridiculous obsession about appearance and his fussing over hair or the cut of a shirt. His need of constant attention eventually making her turn away with a mocking sneer. And when one night he forced other dancers to clear a space so he could show off at centre floor, she wanted to walk away.

But didn't.

Thinking about that performance, especially her part in it, Arlene squirms with shame. She doesn't like who she was with Geoff. She doesn't like who he wanted her to be or what she let herself become. It had never before occurred to her that dancing could be a form of abuse, swirling and carrying her away from herself.

She sees again the five-year-old Amy at the window, hugging the stuffed rabbit given by Geoff and waving goodbye as Arlene folds

herself and her dress into the car. Both mother and child trying to ignore the fact that Arlene is going out for a fourth consecutive night.

"Three's a crowd," Geoff had said.

And always, at least once during those evenings on the dance floor,
a vision of that little face with her rabbit would come to mind, haunt-
ing and sad, and then Arlene would have to twirl faster and harder to
remind herself to feel good about having a night out.

The door opens and Amy comes in. Arlene twists to watch her daughter drop a backpack on the floor and kick off her shoes, padding across
the floor to the fridge. She pours some juice, then digs a folded piece of
paper from her pocket and hands it to Arlene.

"Don't you have anything to say?" Geoff grumbles in her ear. "What
about Amy? Don't you feel bad about what happened to her?"

Arlene takes a deep breath as she unfolds the paper, a permission
slip from school. "I guess I don't see the point now," she replies.

"What do you mean?"

Arlene puts her palm to her forehead and shakes her head.

Geoff keeps going. "If you wanted out, all you had to do ..."

"Who are you talking to?" Amy whispers to her.

Arlene mouths Geoff's name, but Amy looks at her dumbly, unable
to interpret.

"Neil Morton?" Amy frowns.

Arlene shakes her head, No. Her lips exaggerate the shape of his
name: *Geoff.*

"Jack Benson?" Amy's lips curl in a sneer. Names of men Arlene has
dated halfheartedly this past year; men too interested for her interest.

Arlene puts her palm over the telephone mouthpiece and whispers
loudly, "Geoff!"

Amy is thirteen soon. She understands a lot more than Geoff;
certainly more than he gave her credit for. She understands, for instance, why he belittled her for being like he was, a timid, shy, unath-
letic child. And she understands that he held it against her for not being
of his blood.

But now her child-eyes open wide with amazement. "Really?" she asks as she sits, huddling close beside Arlene. She stares alternately at her mother and the phone, incredulous.

Arlene puts her arm around Amy's shoulders and pulls her daughter against her. Amy leans in awkwardly, submitting to the rough hug, then lifts Arlene's hand back over her head and holds it in her lap.

Amy's excitement when Geoff gave her the rabbit; the way he later muttered, "That should keep her quiet for a while."

A shudder crawls up Arlene's spine.

Behind Geoff, Arlene can hear the crooning voice building to a finale: "*We were so good....*"

"Are you coming home for Christmas?" she asks on a whim.

Amy waves her hand in front of Arlene's face. "Tell him we can go skiing!" she whispers.

"I don't know. I don't know if I can," he says.

"*I won't forget you!*" the singer finishes with an upswing.

"You'll probably be able to ski." Arlene is looking out the window as she says this, feeling the dark mountains and the cold sharp in the air. "It was supposed to snow on the mountains this week. It hasn't yet, but it's very cold out there."

April at Whistler, skiing the white, white glare of snow in shorts and T-shirts, the juice of an orange dribbling down Geoff's beard and nobody on the run ahead of them. The mountain all theirs.

Then Amy's bleat behind them on the slope, afraid of the height, afraid of falling, afraid to trust.

"Don't be such a baby!" Geoff's derision echoing off the glacier. Arlene's hard climb back up the slope to soothe the child's panic. "And don't coddle her, Arlene! Christ, she's never going to learn anything with you around!"

Afterward, at dinner, Arlene trying to bring the family back together, throwing questions at both of them to keep the silence at bay, filling the room with talk as she filled their plates. "More salad, Amy? Wasn't that a wonderful last run this afternoon? Didn't she improve, Geoff?

Maybe tomorrow you can teach her to parallel turn. That'd be good, eh, Amy? Two rolls, sweetie?"

"Tell him my last letter came back," Amy insists. "Ask him why."

Arlene looks at her daughter's earnest face and sees again Geoff's last visit: the dog barking hysterically at his unplanned arrival, her own exhaustion after a day of teaching, Amy trying to corner his focus, Geoff wanting only Arlene's attention and none from Amy or the dog, Arlene wanting to be quiet after talking to kids all day, Geoff wanting to discuss money issues, Arlene refusing to talk about selling the house bought with her inheritance.

"Can I talk to him?" Amy holds out her hand towards the receiver.

Arlene looks into her daughter's eyes, sees the blatant need there.

"So ..." Geoff sighs in her ear.

Arlene nods at Amy but looks away.

Amy moves closer, puts a hand on her mother's arm, waiting.

"So ..." Arlene answers.

The background music stops altogether and Arlene can feel a huge emptiness gathering.

"Please!" Amy's anxious face looms in front of her.

Arlene holds up a finger, asking Amy to wait. The girl stands up, paces the length of the room, then comes back, stands above Arlene with arms crossed.

"Okay," Arlene says. She searches for some remorse, but can't find any. There is, instead, a sort of breathless victory, like the end of a fast jive when he'd swing her round and pull her back.

This dance is over.

Amy puts her hand over her mom's on the receiver and Arlene raises her eyes to her daughter once again. Behind Amy she sees the photo of that small child with the big telephone, listening; waiting.

"Hang on a sec," Arlene says and relinquishes the receiver. But as Amy takes it, Arlene drops her hand onto the phone's cradle, sliding her thumb over the reset button and pressing firmly. Three seconds, four maybe.

"Hello?" Amy's voice is tight, almost a squeak. "Hello ...?" Arlene watches from the side as Amy's throat seems to swallow. When she turns back to her mother, the girl's eyes have narrowed into thin lines. "He hung up! Didn't he want to talk to me? At all?"

Arlene holds out her hand to her daughter's hurt.

"What a turd!" Amy spits out the word. She throws the receiver onto the linoleum floor and flings herself from the room. Arlene stares at the phone as it lies there without static.

She sits for a minute, maybe longer, then gets up and goes to the front door. As she opens it, the blast of arctic air feels familiar.

When the music stopped they'd step into the night outside and the coolness spilling over her sweat-dampened skin would make her tremble.

Like she does now.

The Forest, The Trees

When Ben talks about his dark theory of love, she is not really listening. She's swallowed up by his eyes, large as a deer's, liquid and deep. She thinks how she could swim in them if he'd let her.

"We fall in love with people who don't love us back," he says. "And they usually want someone who doesn't want them either. It's some kind of karmic joke or something."

She smiles, but not at his words. She is studying his eyelashes, the way they curl as thick as the undergrowth in the forest behind her house.

Ben gives her a look full of chagrin. "It's always the dweebs—the ones we could care less about—that fall in love with us." He shakes his head and looks out the window at the ocean.

Ben is one of her new neighbours, living with his widowed mom since his recent divorce. They met on the beach nearby and ever since then he's been visiting her in the evenings, walking down the street to sit and talk for hours about his ex-wife and his kids. She listens and makes appropriately sympathetic noises because she knows that after all the anger has blown over, Ben will need someone to help him heal. What she's thinking is that maybe when that happens, the two of them can get together, go somewhere.

He does things that touch her without even realizing the effect. One Sunday he shows up with his chainsaw, ready to fall a dead tree in her yard. He arrives dressed in his work clothes: logger's hard hat, eye goggles, those too-short jeans with the lead-lined legs held up by orange Husqvarna suspenders and leather work gloves. While he operates the saw, she observes the pure maleness of his body: the dark shadow of beard, unshaved because it is the weekend; the strain of muscle on his thighs and buttocks and the hard ridge of abdominal wall beneath his T-shirt. It is all she can do not to go to him, touch his arm so he'll shut down the saw and she can drag him inside.

But her fantasies are interrupted by real life. In the midst of the screaming noise, Ben's mother walks up the road to watch with her. They chat amiably, she and the older woman, each admiring Ben from their own points of view, and the thought enters her head that the scene in her garden is not unlike that of a TV sitcom. How else could she be good friends with the mother of a man whose lights she wants to screw out?

Today, though, she takes Ben's dark theory and files it away at the back of her mind. She ignores what he says about love and follows his stare out the window, thinks about how harsh the water looks out there. She came to this place from the city, wanting to be near the water, but now she sees how the steel blue and dark grey of ocean opposes the warm green of forest.

A month after felling her tree, Ben's conversations shift focus. He begins to tell stories of women coming on to him or of a physical encounter with someone he doesn't want. Then he tells her about someone in his boss's office, a woman he thinks is pretty hot, and she wonders why he's telling her about his sex life. She wonders why he doesn't offer to make her come instead of telling her about all the women who've made him come and she hopes it's his clumsy logger's way of flirting.

Now when he calls to say he's coming over, she slips into the bathroom to get ready, puts on some mascara or perfume. She's still listening to all his complaints and stories, but what she really hopes is that she'll get laid.

It's been a decade since her last love affair, followed by a number of sorry little flings, and the grind of time is working against her. She's not desperate—yet—and anyway, if it comes to that there are already two of those dweebs hanging around her door. No, not desperate, but when she sees Ben standing in the doorway, her heart rate jumps as though she's just done a line of coke.

In spite of the mush her innards turn to when Ben is around, her brains aren't yet entirely deteriorated. Now, listening to his talk about himself and his job and his women and his life, she begins to yawn openly. But whenever she tries to redirect him, steering the conversation towards subjects with more emotional reality, Ben turns pointedly away. She finds herself thinking how remarkably one-sided this relationship is, how completely lacking in two-way communication.

She makes two decisions: (1) It doesn't matter that he can't talk as long as he can make love; (2) If he can't make love, then the issue is dead all round. Literally and emotionally, like their conversations.

And once she makes that decision, what happens next is her own fault.

As soon as Ben starts up again, complaining about how hard it is to find a partner, doesn't he deserve someone nice, at least someone to sleep with, she doesn't miss a beat.

"Why can't two friends have sex together?"

At first Ben stares at her. Then he relaxes, interested, and she releases a soft breath of air.

But it's likely the word "friends" that cinches the proposition, because Ben doesn't do anything without thinking about it first. He keeps sex in its place, love in an entirely different place.

After that first physical encounter, Ben doesn't come by for a whole week and she finds out again how much more than sex there is to want from a man. Especially a man like Ben, who knows how to build things and who thinks about the way it should be done; who has a drawing power that he isn't even aware of. It's in the way his muscles ripple like a bodybuilder's and the way he's so tired after a day of physical labour that he falls asleep with one rough hand on a woman's belly, making her feel marked. Or as though he might love her.

She spends that long week full of seething, but when he shows up again, she puts on a smile. This time when he leaves, she is restless and unable to focus. She tries walking the length of the beach to calm herself, but halfway along, the ocean feels too open, too wide, so she climbs the hill behind and heads into the dense greenery of forest. Above the water, she is cocooned by the waving boughs of firs, cedars, hemlocks. Now the overhead sky is a warm green blanket and the tangled branches beneath her feet are the paws of a kitten batting at her boots. She feels captured, safe.

She tells herself that what she's done with Ben isn't such a big problem, not unless Mr. Right comes along. But the guy on the white horse hasn't been seen in almost twenty years and so she makes a resolution: until that guy shows, Ben can fill in.

She replays bits of monologues from Ben's endlessly self-absorbed conversations about his marriage, and she decides that he is not at all as he likes to present himself: cold, tough, heartless. She knows, because she has been witness, that this man can cry as well as protect, use his hands to make a home and take it apart. And if he can do all those things, surely there is more beneath his dense surface.

Without intent, Ben gives her no-occasion gifts, birthday and Christmas cards signed Love Ben at the bottom. She takes these small offerings as proof that love, or a primitive form of it, lurks somewhere beneath the uncommitted exterior. She hopes he has forgotten about the dweeb-factor, how only the wrong kind of person falls in love with him.

Now she daydreams about spending her life with him. This in spite of the fact that Ben's made things abundantly clear about himself: he's a logger and all he wants is a good meal on the table at night and a good lay in the bedroom and no hassles from Anywoman about anything. And as if to further undermine her dreams, within a week of starting on a new clearcut he phones to tell her that the local bar is a good meat market.

She tries to ignore how remarkably quiet her friends become when she mentions Ben's name.

"What's in this for you?" they want to know.

It is not a question she wishes to ask herself and so she looks away, insinuating that the answer should be obvious. "If you want something enough," she says, "you have to be willing to walk through a minefield for it."

After a year has passed, it makes no difference whether she turns back or continues to cross the minefield. Either way is lethal.

She begins to feel the tight walls of her prison. There is no one to whom she can admit how long it's been since she and Ben have been together, or share something said the last time he was home, something from which she's constructed a much deeper meaning than intended. This is what it's like to live in a small community, she thinks: sleeping with your neighbour on Friday night, then taking his mother to the farmer's market Saturday morning. Doing both without being able to discuss the existence of love.

The next time Ben comes home, she tries a verbal nudge: after sex one night, she tells him she loves him.

"Aw, don't," he says, pulling away.

But she holds on to his hand.

"I don't mean I love you and I want to get married, Ben. I only mean you're important to me."

But it's as though the forest has cast a spell on her, the way she still doesn't know how to talk to this man. This time it takes several weeks to persuade him that it is safe to come back; it was just her hormones acting up.

One night she lies in the dark, listening to the slowing of their two breaths, the way they change from heavy gasping to steady pants and then a regular in and out of air. She is enjoying just being there with him, feeling the rise and fall of his chest under her ear and the warmth of his bigger, rougher palm against hers, when out of nowhere he says: "Are you happy?"

And because she is afraid that he will change his mind about wanting to know something about her, that then she will have lost an opportunity to connect with him, she rushes to answer.

"Really happy," she says, nodding. Without stopping to wonder, without even checking: Am I happy?

She waits for another minute, making her breath more and more shallow, listening to see if his burst of conversation—if that's what it is—will continue, but nothing more comes. When she realizes she is holding her breath, she takes a large gulp of air and lifts her head, peering for his face in the dark.

"Why?" she asks.

But the moment is gone. He's already sitting up and reaching for his socks.

In the cold of the open doorway, she stands to receive his good-night hug and then he walks away. She stares up at the black sky pricked with stars, listening for the slam of the gate that says he is gone.

Burrowing into the tangle of sheets on her empty bed once more, she replays that fleeting moment.

Are you happy?

This time the words bring an unbidden image: a drive in her father's car when she was very small, a stop at the candy store, and that same question afterwards, "Are you happy now?" The peeved tone with which it was asked.

She closes her eyes and shakes her head. Surely Ben's question meant, "Do I make you happy?"

After a while, unable to settle, she gets up and heads for the fluorescent shock of the bathroom. As she passes the mirror, she stops in recognition, the face of a dweeb reflected back at her.

Where Love Goes

The two women hug as though it has been three years, not three
weeks, since their last coffee together.

"Latte?" Dana asks as she strips off her coat. And while she
goes for the coffee, Adrienne sinks into the clatter and steam of the
espresso bar, the warm hum of conversation around her. She feels safely
hidden, tucked away beside all the other customers red-faced from the
out-of-doors, their cold hands wrapped around coffee mugs and coats
draped hastily on chair backs.

When Dana comes back with two lattes, she slips into her seat and
leans forward. "Wait 'til you hear what we did last night!"

For the past month Dana has been involved with a soccer player
whose team practises in the park behind her house. Dari is a recent im-
migrant with poor English but the language problems haven't hindered
other forms of communication. Now Dana tells Adrienne about their
latest sexual foray.

"I never even *talked* about stuff like this with Rick!" Her voice is squeezed with excitement.

Adrienne pictures Dana's ex-husband, wonders what Rick would say about this clandestine affair. No doubt he would be horrified, like the soccer player's Muslim family, by Dana's dark-of-the-night encounters with a man twenty years her junior and a different coloured skin. He would probably suggest, as other friends have, that divorce should make a woman untouchable in some invisible but indelible way.

"Funny," Dana muses more calmly, "sex was one thing I never missed 'til Dari came along."

The sparkle of Christmas lights outside reflect in Dana's eyes and Adrienne turns her head to take in the winking haze across the city's darkening skyline.

"So," Dana says eventually. "How was it?"

Adrienne lifts her latte and blows at the froth, catches Dana's grey eyes staring at her.

"A little disappointing," she says when she lowers the cup.

Dana's eyes are blank when she nods. She sits back in her chair and crosses one leg over the other, waiting.

Sometimes it is unnerving as hell to have a psychologist for a friend. Dana's ability to outline clear-cut parameters regularly makes Adrienne feel childish and naïve about her own fuzzy boundaries. Right now, for instance, she would like to be able to ask for concrete advice, but the thought that Dana would never allow a messy situation like hers makes Adrienne squirm.

She blows at her latte again and concentrates on swirling the stir stick. She glances around at the noise and bustle of the coffee bar before shrugging. "I really fucked up."

Dana's eyebrows lift in inquiry.

Adrienne sighs. "I should have known better."

Her eyes fixed on Adrienne, Dana leans forward to sip at her coffee. After a pause she asks, "What are you going to do?"

Adrienne shakes her head, puts a hand to her brow and worries the skin there. "I just wish—"

"What?"

"Whatever—it's too late now."

Across the table Dana waits patiently, offering an expanse of empty time. When Adrienne doesn't bite, Dana suggests a starting point.

"Anyone can have bad sex. It's the electric stuff that's hard to find." She laughs, a small breath of air like a pant.

Adrienne shivers at the sound. And for the tiniest instant she is back in bed with Mark, sandwiched between his thick body and the heat of the duvet. She feels the press of mattress beneath her spine and the ceiling of blackness overhead as she lies squeezed between Mark's confident snoring and her own spiralling thoughts.

The whole thing had begun with an e-mail, a silly, half-joking invitation about a cheap charter to Mexico.

I haven't been on a real holiday in over ten years, Adrienne wrote to him. *Want to go with me?*

And the response from her childhood, then teenage, now mid-life friend, was pointed: *Are you coming on to me?*

A warm dizziness had rolled down Adrienne's neck into the cavern of her body. As though a part of her had heaved a great sigh of relief, Adrienne relaxed some long-kept vigil and smiled at the computer screen.

Now she thinks she must have been carried away because of Mark's Scandinavian eyes. If those ice-blue irises had been right in front of her while she typed, not somewhere out in cyberspace, maybe then she'd have recognized her delusion. Instead she'd stepped right into a trap of her own making.

Maybe I am coming on to you, she responded to Mark's question. *Is that a problem?*

For a week, two or three times a night they had e-mailed each other, prying tentatively at first, then graduating to more direct questions. *How are you feeling with this? When did you know? Are you as scared as I am?* Opening up as though they were a couple in the counsellor's office.

In Mark's company Adrienne could be her unpretentious self. Once he had dropped by without warning on the first day of her period. She lay on the couch, tired, crampy, miserable.

"You look like shit," he said, bending to give her a hug.

"Same to you."

"Want me to make you a cup of tea?"

Later, after massaging her feet, he had filled a hot water bottle, tucked it against her belly, and kissed her goodbye on the cheek. Adrienne slumped into a dazed sleep without ever noticing how easily the afternoon had passed.

To the woman who became his wife, Mark once announced, "Adrienne can be a real bitch." And then he added, "But she's the most up-front person I know. Incredibly responsive."

"I was scared shitless to meet you after that," Mark's wife told her when they met.

Adrienne shook her head. "No wonder."

Mark's comment had both stung and warmed her and she carried it in her thoughts for a long time, remembering it at strange moments. The words became a kind of mantra—*She's the most up-front person I know*—and in the end they were what emboldened her to approach Mark.

But Adrienne had felt no telltale electric shiver, none of the dangerous thrills so common during the new stages of other encounters. She told herself it was because Mark was a calming influence; that her body was unfamiliar with the company of someone safe.

Outside the espresso bar, the grey marine of a west coast winter drizzles down the windows. Adrienne watches a red and yellow tug trying to manoeuvre between two others at the pier. The black rubber gunwales jostle the dock and quick puffs of smoke blast from the funnel as the throbbing diesel rocks the vessel back and forth. From the wheelhouse a heavy-set bearded man, a Captain Highliner type, cranes his neck to see through the rain.

Adrienne turns back to Dana. "Did you read *Clan of the Cave Bear?*"

"*You* read that?"

"Remember the scene where Jondalar visits some other clan and one of the elders approaches him to ask if he'd be willing to do the honour of initiating a young virgin?"

"Mmhmm." Dana sips her coffee. "Juicy stuff."

Adrienne's eyebrows lift as she nods. "Wouldn't it have been great if our first lovers had been like that? We'd have been so much better at choosing mates."

Dana smiles at her. "You're asking why you can't have John's personality with Jack's jewels?"

"Well, why can't I?" Adrienne sighs. "You know, the last time I had good sex was with Brad. Remember him?" A thirty-year-old handyman who was supposed to repair her leaky roof and who afterward ended up in her bed, his tanned skin glistening next to hers as they worked up a sweat in the late summer sun. It was the kind of affair to which Adrienne was so prone, the kind that exploded out of control, then fizzled with the watery death of a firecracker hitting damp earth.

Dana chuckles. "You mean Bad Brad?"

Adrienne grins at the nickname. "If I'd known he was going to be my last great lay, I'd have made more out of the opportunity."

Dana splutters into her latte, bending forward to put down the cup and reach for a serviette.

"Seriously." Adrienne watches Dana wiping the foam from her upper lip. "How do you know if it's going to be your last-ever screw? Ever thought of that?"

Dana's turkey neck wobbles when she shakes her head, and Adrienne's hand lifts in response, feels for bulges beneath her own chin. Her eyes take in the grey at Dana's temples: mid-life was no longer some nebulous date in the distant future.

Dana finishes her coffee and stands up. "Gotta get back to work, girl." She pauses as she starts to leave, puts a hand on Adrienne's shoulder. "Most things rarely turn out the way we wish."

"Really?" Adrienne says with patent sarcasm.

Dana leans to hug her. "Go easy on him."

Adrienne watches out the window as Captain Highliner uses his whole body to coil a rope as thick as a boa constrictor. She holds her mug in front of her face and admires the thick grey hair, curly like Mark's, and his much stockier body. And when he turns and laughs at a crew mate, she imagines a much deeper voice.

After all their carefully constructed e-mails, Mark's voice on the phone had soothed her into believing they could move to a higher level. Mesmerized by his calm, Adrienne began to have out-of-the-ordinary thoughts about her friend—how his voice would sound next to her ear, the heat of his breath against her cheek or the rough scrape of beard on her stomach. The fantasies had brought a light to the deep night of her winter: Adrienne wanted to believe that Mark had always been her soulmate.

They juggled their calendars to find a date to get together and then they waited for the day to arrive. Consumed by the slow progress of time, Adrienne began to feel as though she were on a conveyor belt en route to the Moment of Truth. But she withheld any confession from Dana. She wanted to hide the warmth of this secret in her belly, to be alone with its presence like a mother's first knowledge of conception. Until she knew whether the date would turn into anything, she did not want to share her dreams and fantasies about it.

She tried not to think about how she and Mark would get from the hug of greeting to the bedroom. During their late-night phone conversations, they had made small, joking references to the fact that they were going to sleep together

"I hope you don't snore," she worried.

"I don't think so," he laughed. "Do you?"

Adrienne was relying on the assumption that Mark, also divorced for a number of years, would be as sex-starved as she was. It seemed like a win-win situation: the history was already in place and the sex would be a mutual bonus. Given time, everything would unfold naturally.

Leaving the espresso bar, Adrienne points her car into the heavy traffic beneath the splash of lit-up office towers. The lanes of rush-hour vehicles are feisty, bucking and jerking like rodeo bulls as they start and stop, inching forward, then braking. The festive demands of Christmas seem to have affected the entire city, and Adrienne watches, horrified, as a glowering man beside her ploughs into the car in front of him, slams his car into PARK and leaps out cursing. He leaves his door open and gives the finger to those whose horns bleat mercilessly. Glancing over her shoulder, Adrienne gauges whether she can squeeze into the next lane, escape the inevitable traffic snarl resulting from this fender-bender, but she is already sandwiched by SUVs and buses.

She leans her forehead against the steering wheel. The shrinking daylight and the cold outside increase her longing to be at home, curled in front of the fire with a blanket. The solstice approaches and Adrienne's entire body resists the effort of being out in the dark at this time of year, wanting to hibernate until spring. She thinks how cavemen had it right, living according to instinctual responses, and then she thinks about sleeping beneath an animal skin, trapped beside the body heat of someone else throughout those long winter nights.

The image takes her back to that night with Mark and she relives the disastrous session, replaying the events that had delivered her naked to him. She'd had to crawl to the living room couch to find a few hours' sleep and now she wonders if he too recognized the non-success of that night together. She considers the possibility that Mark felt as stupid as she did.

But when she reviews his goodbye kiss, the way his lips had met hers and his tongue had probed her mouth, lingering there a little too long to be understood as anything less than heightened interest, she sighs.

An hour later, Adrienne battles the human traffic·in the mall, fighting her way towards the escalator of a large department store. She rides to the second floor, men's wear, and wanders among the displays. After fifteen minutes of browsing, she realizes that a suitable gift is going to cost more than she wants to spend, but the nagging sensation that she is somehow at fault—that she owes Mark—leaves her guilt-ridden and determined to correct the error.

She rifles through a display of handknit sweaters, lays two of them flat and stands back. Trying to visualize Mark in the bulky merino, she spends several tired minutes of indecision, then picks up the other. She takes the dark multicolour design with a $150 price tag on the collar towards the cash register.

Two teenaged girls stand in line before her. One of them holds up a leather-look g-string to admire. "I'll give it to him on Christmas Eve so he can model it!" she trills for the benefit of other customers. "Not that it'll stay on for very long."

Her friend glances sideways at Adrienne, then looks away. Adrienne notices something red and shiny in the other girl's hand. The thought occurs to her that the two of them have gone shopping for their "men;" that one of them—probably the leather-look one—has talked the other into buying gifts to titillate their sex lives.

"Excuse me?" a voice retrieves Adrienne's attention. The young cashier stares at her in frustration. "Will that be cash or charge?"

"Charge, please." Adrienne hands her card over and turns away, trying to avoid the huff of impatient shoppers behind her. Her eyes find the two g-string girls standing in the aisle, worrying about whether to eat now or later. Adrienne scrutinizes their tiny waists and the way their negligible breasts sit lightly, as though barely attached to their bodies.

"Seventeen—*maybe*," she thinks with a sneer. And as soon as the thought occurs, Adrienne is shamed by its harshness. She remembers being like these two, young and wanting to disguise her age. She too had coated her eyes with black eyeliner and dark eyeshadow in an unsophisticated attempt to attract the attention, and desire, of the opposite sex.

The cashier almost shoves the pen in her hand. When Adrienne returns it, she recites, "Happy holidays, ma'am."

Adrienne flinches at the insincerity of the wish and the equally unwanted title. When she reaches across the counter for her bag, she notices how the cashier is already stretching past her for the next purchase.

On the escalator down, Adrienne surveys the Christmas scene below, the shoppers framed by colours, lights and noise. Her eyes catch on a young couple, the boy red-headed and burly, an athlete perhaps, while the girl is so dainty as to be fragile, the blackest hair above a translucent complexion. They stop in front of the jewellery display, leaning into each other with complete abandon, arms around waists, parcels and bundles at their sides like saddlebags.

The girl lays her head on the boy's thick shoulder and Adrienne's smile is reflexive. Stepping off the escalator, she slows her pace as she approaches the young couple. She sees the boy put down his bags without letting go of the girl's waist, his strong wrist exposed when he reaches a long arm across the counter for a ring held by the clerk.

Without warning, Adrienne is jostled from behind and the two girls from the men's wear department swerve past her, one pointing at the young couple and the other blowing a balloon-sized bubble of gum. They stop right behind the couple and Leather-Look reaches a hand up and over the boy's shoulder to point.

"This one, Pete. It'll make your wang look much bigger!" The two girls whoop, then careen into the crowd, laughing loudly.

Faces turn to stare and Adrienne, near the scene of the crime, feels the focus of their accusatory glares. She swivels and, as she does, catches sight of a familiar figure on the other side of the jewellery case. Mark, so close he could reach her in three strides.

Adrienne spins the other way, heads down the next aisle. From behind the safety of a high shelf, she glances back to see if he has spotted her.

Mark is shaking his head and laughing with the two lovers, leaning on his arms as though he were standing at the bar with good friends. She can see the trademark plaid scarf around his neck, the soft mole on his cheek.

A sales clerk approaches and Mark points to the case in front of him. The employee unlocks the door and lifts out two gold chains, both gaudy and overpowering, the kind favoured by older, heavier women. Mark reaches for the chunkier necklace and Adrienne frowns.

As if aware of her reaction, Mark lays the chain on the velvet mat in front of him. He points to another item in the case and the clerk retrieves it. Cradling the new chain in her hands, she holds the end with the clasp to her shoulder and lets it drape across her chest for Mark's approval. Adrienne sees a stone embedded in the centre of the chain—something sparkling—and bites her lip.

The clerk places the chain with the stone beside the other on the mat as Mark points once more at the case. This time she picks up an elaborate twisting of gold and silver, simple but exquisite, and Adrienne holds her breath. Yes, that one, she thinks, before a hot blush of shame hurries her toward the exit.

She is locking her car outside the house when a thought too obviously overlooked makes her heart drop. What if Mark's impotence was *because* of her? Now, though the progressively shrinking hours of daylight will soon reverse and she will be able to mark the lengthening of each day, Adrienne is filled with the idea that this winter is one of the darkest ever.

She picks up the phone to call Dana, purposefully lightening her tone as she asks, "Want to have a drink with us Christmas Eve?"

There is a slight pause before Dana answers, "Are you worried about being alone with him?"

"Please will you come?"

"Not this time. You need to do this by yourself."

Dana had called Adrienne the night before the big date with Mark. "I just wanted to tell you that Mark called," she said in a low voice. "I thought you should know that I know."

The words had seeped into Adrienne's awareness like the slow burn of Novocaine, their long sustain echoing inside her skull for what seemed like minutes. She sat down, overwhelmed by the thought that Mark had betrayed her.

He must have needed to crow to someone; or maybe he'd assumed Adrienne had already told Dana.

Adrienne felt deflated, her balloon of fantasy punctured. After a moment, the true meaning of Dana's announcement—despite her carefully chosen words delivered in a soft voice—hit home: *Are you thinking straight?*

It was like the slash of a hockey stick to the back of the knee and Adrienne crumpled at the blow. She hung up the phone and went to lie down, a cool face cloth over her eyes. An hour later she bristled: why did Dana think it was okay to pass judgment on her?

With rekindled determination, Adrienne raged through the house, slamming cupboard doors and yanking laundry from the dryer, venting her disbelief. "Bitch!" Snapping the towels and sheets with a sharp ferocity. "Unbelievable conceit!" Later, unloading the dishwasher, it came to her while crashing dishes on the counter that what bothered her most was feeling cornered by her actions. That Dana might be right.

In that instant she felt exposed as a fraud. Not because she had failed to be something she couldn't, but because she had the gall to try.

Adrienne chews the end of her pen as she stares out the window at the neighbourhood's Christmas decorations. She turns back to her desk, bending over a card to write. Her lips move as she reads the words to herself but then she grimaces and tears it up. She stands, goes to the kitchen and pours a drink. On her way back, she stops before a bulletin board covered in photos, a collection begun years ago by her now-grown-and-gone daughter.

They are mostly photos of that same child, a progression of shots from a toothless infant to the college graduate of five years ago. And in the middle, its corners curling, an old black and white class photo from Adrienne's kindergarten days.

An arrow inked on the photo points to Adrienne's five-year-old self sitting cross-legged, gap-toothed and pigtailed, on the floor. One row back, another arrow points to a chubby and curly-haired Mark standing with his hands clasped and wearing a bow tie. Both children lightly freckled across the nose, their smiles—hers wide and precocious and his quiet and shy—revealing their personalities.

Adrienne's index finger reaches out to the smiling boy in the photo. Though she doesn't remember those years or that little boy very well, she is comforted by the knowledge that he has been standing behind her for so long.

Mark arrives with a bottle of wine in hand. He leans inside the doorway, claims such a strong kiss that Adrienne closes her eyes, trying not to feel the pit of shame in her gut, the horror of disbelief that he doesn't sense what is coming.

When he gives her the velvet-covered box, her heart sinks. It is smaller, even, than the box that should have contained one of the gold chains. The gruelling thought occurs to her that he may have bought her something else, something of more profound intent, and that if he has, she will be in a deeper grip than that of winter.

Adrienne carries the velvet box into the living room and Mark follows her. She puts the small box on the coffee table, then picks up the wrapped sweater and turns to offer it.

"For you," she smiles.

He squeezes the parcel. "Well, at least it's not a book." He grins and sits on the couch. She sits beside him and watches as he tears off the paper. The wrapping with its gift tag falls to the floor.

Adrienne retrieves the tag while Mark pulls out the sweater. He stands up to try it on.

"Nice."

"Like it?"

"It's beautiful. Perfect fit."

"You forgot the card." Adrienne holds it out to him.

Mark sits down. He kisses her cheek as he takes the card then digs in a pocket for his glasses.

And as her old friend reads, Adrienne watches his face. She sees the frown and then the raised eyebrows before he lays the card on the table. She waits until Mark turns to her and then she touches her fingers to his cheek, holding his gaze. She finds her reflection in the pale blue of his eyes and she is grateful for what is missing there: the slow burn of yearning and the quiet camouflage of lies.

"I let myself get carried away by a child's fantasy," she says when she sees him waiting. "That dumb happily-ever-after syndrome."

"Is that what THANKS FOR TRYING means?"

"I'm being honest, Marko. It's what you always said you liked about me."

Mark shakes his head at the floor. He brings his hands together and flexes the intertwined fingers and then he stands up.

"Can we at least talk about it?" she says as he heads for the door.

"Just let me lick my wounds for now, Adrienne. I'm not up for making you feel better."

As the door shuts heavily, Adrienne sees the velvet-covered box on the coffee table. She picks it up and holds it for a minute then stands to put it on the bookshelf, turning toward the windows and the distant mountains rising dark against the black night sky.

Outside, she knows, the winter carries spring in its womb.

Things You Don't Know About Goldfish

The summer mosquitoes made sitting in Aislyn's backyard a chore.

"Build a fish pond," says Stella in her gravelly voice, adding, "Fish love mosquitoes."

Aislyn mentions the idea to her husband. "What would a maintenance person know about it?" Dick sneers. "Especially a dyke?"

Dick is an instructor at another campus. There, the repairs and maintenance are done by a man.

A year after the fish pond suggestion, Dick leaves Aislyn for his teaching assistant, a young Asian whose breasts and body are so tiny that her smallness makes Aislyn feel top-heavy and old. The weekend after his departure, Aislyn carries a spade into her backyard and digs a hole for a pond.

She goes to the pet store, walking down aisles of gurgling fish tanks and peering into their watery depths for the shiny orange fish. Row after row is filled with exotics—fluttery fighting fish, elegant angels, miniature neons and tetras—and after several minutes a thought occurs: Why would you choose the ordinary when you could have the exotic?

She approaches the clerk at the counter about goldfish. He jerks a thumb over his shoulder and Aislyn notices, then, the clear plastic hoses running in and out of big blue barrels. She moves towards them and leans over the edge of the nearest barrel to find hordes of golden fish swimming in mad circles.

"Feed for the bigger fish," the clerk says.

Aislyn looks up questioningly. The young man draws a finger across his neck and she understands: this stark blue corral is a holding pen before the fish abattoir.

"I want four," she says.

She feels no superior morals about saving the fish from a worse fate, but as she watches the clerk scooping her chosen four into a small plastic bag, Aislyn believes they are going to a far better place.

What she isn't prepared for is the piercing concern that takes root when her aquiline charges are poured into the dark waters of their new home. Throughout the first week, Aislyn finds herself drawn to the window overlooking the pond, watching for a bright flash of wavy fins. Whenever they dart out of the shadows, she smiles and relaxes her shoulders, goes back to her computer. But soon she gets up again, looking for a snack or a drink, any excuse to check and make sure her fish are still alive.

Being rescued from the blue barrel of hopelessness should inspire some sort of happiness, Aislyn believes. She watches for evidence of fishy glee, but the passing of each day reveals nothing new about their behaviour. The fish come out of their depths according to some unfathomable whim, kissing the pond's surface with their sucking mouths on a schedule Aislyn cannot predict.

When at the end of the first week the fish cannot be found, Aislyn spends days fretting over whether they've been eaten by a heron or a raccoon. She goes back to the pet store, buys some flakes to scatter across the pond's surface, then waits for her fish to show. After a few minutes, thinking her shadow may be alarming, she steps away from the pond's edge. No fish appear. Aislyn retires inside and resumes her place at the window, waiting.

She worries about them to neighbours and her concern becomes a source of their teasing. Her fish, they jibe, are stand-in children. Even her sister jokes about her late motherhood experience, phoning to ask, "How's Mickey Finn doing, Lynnie?"

In the summer, Aislyn invites Stella to come see the result of her suggestion. At first they sit in the sun on the front stoop, discussing mutual work acquaintances, then mutual interests, and finally mutual experiences. An hour later, after they've relaxed into a comfort zone, Stella turns searchingly to Aislyn.

"How did you know when your marriage was over?"

Aislyn hears the pinched tone in Stella's deep voice but does not look at her. Instead, she remembers their last conversation at work.

"How's things?" Aislyn had asked.

Stella shook her head as she looked away. "Kind of tense at home," she said.

Aislyn nodded sympathetically, but resisted asking. Stella lived with another woman and lesbians seemed like foreign territory to Aislyn.

Now, when she looks at Stella, she is struck by the lines of pain on the woman's usually strong countenance. Her head droops like a heavy sunflower, as though her neck can no longer support the weight of her thoughts. Her olive-skinned face is hidden by a voluminous cloud of wiry black hair.

The sun catches in the rich, black kinks and Aislyn is mesmerized by the effect. She wants to reach out and touch, see if the haze of hair feels the way it looks—like steel wool—before Stella asks again.

"Or was it a surprise?" Her proud forehead is frowning.

Aislyn looks away from her black eyes, stares across the street. "You just know," she says. "Maybe not 'til after the fact, but the warning signs are all there."

She can feel Stella's persistent stare on the side of her face, but a prickliness in her gut, a fear hovering beneath her skin, prevents her from meeting that look. How would she know, if she saw an invitation there, which to acknowledge: her own hesitation or Stella's magnetism?

Aislyn knows she is naïve about lots of things, but particularly about lesbians and lesbian sex. She would like to ask how they do it and whether the same partner always performs the male role. Whether Stella was the male or the female in her partnership.

She would like to ask, but she does not want to offend, nor does she want to be laughed at. She suspects that she should know the answers—she has a PhD, after all—but how would you find out about that sort of thing unless you knew someone from the other side of the fence? Or you went over the fence.

Frightened by such an idea, Aislyn prefers to avoid any talk about fantasies, especially of the female sexual variety. Right now the idea of being touched by a woman makes the skin on the back of her thighs shrink, her stomach flip.

She had once vehemently agreed with Dick when he proclaimed, "Dykes don't have the right equipment." Having a partner at the time had made Aislyn smugly secure. Now, though, she felt precariously single and unclaimed.

But Stella is anxious about other things. "Was it a surprise?" she asks again.

Aislyn stares at the haloed rays of the sun behind a tall fir tree before sitting forward to rest her forearms on her knees. She lowers her eyes to the concrete and watches an ant scurrying about, sees the way it explores every pit in the cracked stairs, the way it struggles to drag the corpse of a woodbug the entire length of her foot.

When she turns back, she sees the redness in Stella's soulful eyes. In Aislyn's stomach is a sickening clump of memories from those last desperate weeks before separation.

She takes a deep breath, then sits up. "You stay out as long as you can because you don't want to go home." She stares at the space in front of her, unseeing. "And when you do go home, you wait outside, too afraid to go in." She turns to look at Stella. "And if he's there when you open the door, there's that awkward silence after the 'Hi,' and both of you look away after the least possible eye contact."

Stella bends forward to pick up a twig. "He?" she smirks.

Aislyn grimaces in acknowledgement of her slip. "He, she. And every room in the place feels too small when you're both at home. Or everything they do bugs you: the way they wash a dish as soon as it's used or they never take their shoes off when they come in, leaving sand and dirt everywhere." She turns to look right at Stella. "You know?"

Stella nods slightly.

"And the things you used to find endearing—like the way they make lists of things to do and then don't do any of them, or the way they talk baby talk to the dog...."

Stella pokes at the ant with the twig. "Is that what he did?"

Aislyn rests her elbows behind her and leans her weight on them. She looks down at her dangling fingers and sees the heavily lined backs of her hands. She wonders when her body grew so ancient-looking and whether the rest of the world sees her as old all of a sudden, and then she raises her eyes to Stella, sees her sad, waiting stare. "I only figured all that out after he left. After I could breathe again."

Those long nights wrapped in a blanket on the living room sofa, not wanting to sleep beside his warmth after his offhand conversation over dinner. The evenings spent laughing and chatting with friends as though her life were routine, normal, fine; not wanting to admit how grim the reality was. The plaguing fears about what would happen to her—Where would she live? Who would take care of her?—as if becoming single again was as difficult to survive as cancer. And the thought that had haunted her most continuously, the most ridiculous and most real of them all: *What if no one ever wants me again?*

Aislyn peeks at Stella, sees the incongruity of the teary face on such a sturdy body. She imagines putting her arm around those broad shoulders, laying that glorious head of hair against her cheek and making soothing noises while stroking the kinky waves. But her arm stays at her side; her friend remains unconsoled.

Now, from the safety of the other side, Aislyn considers the possibility that Stella's domain may be less foreign than she has assumed. Still, she clings to the shield she has raised before her, holding firm in case the exotic reaches of Lesbos are somehow capable of luring—and tainting—her.

But her mind betrays her with a vision of two women naked together, and for a moment Aislyn imagines herself entwined with Stella. Almost immediately, the skin on her thighs tightens in a horrified recognition of where she has gone.

What worries Aislyn most is the realization that her fear might signify a craving. Might make *her* into what Dick called Stella: "Some kind of aberration."

Stella stands up. She puts her hands in her shorts' pockets, a gesture that Aislyn reads as notice of impending departure.

Against the evening light, Stella's silhouette is full and complete, the embodiment of another kind of femininity. Next to her, Aislyn feels the solidity of her own presence.

Stella puts her hands on her thick Mediterranean hips and Aislyn is suddenly aware that she is staring at the well-fleshed legs of her friend. Staring at them as if they were utterly naked.

"I forgot about the fish." Aislyn stands and heads for the backyard, not waiting for Stella's response.

The water is dark and murky, almost boggy. Aislyn leans over the pond. Behind her she feels Stella's close presence, and they stand together quietly, waiting for a tell-tale flash of gold.

"Are you sure there are fish in there?" Stella jokes after a long minute of peering into the dark water.

"Three. Had four, but one died."

"Well, they must be in their fatigues, then. Can't see anything gold or orange in there."

"They take their time, y'know. Can't be too careful with the kind of visitors you get around here."

Stella's laugh is a husky bark, and she punches Aislyn playfully. Aislyn smiles inquisitively and Stella shakes her head. "Is that what you're feeling with me around?"

Aislyn feels the flush on her cheeks as she crouches at the pond's edge.

In the next moment, Stella's hand is warm and solid on her shoulder. The touch is comforting, not alarming, and Aislyn waits to see what will happen. But Stella removes her hand and leaves an emptiness there, a sudden cold as though part of Aislyn has been violated, left naked and exposed to the weather.

Stella squats beside her, sticks a finger into the murky pond and swirls it lightly. "Here fishy, fishy," her deep voice croons. And then she asks, "Do they have names?"

Aislyn shakes her head. "I wasn't sure they'd live." She points her chin at the pond. "They're probably hiding in the pipe. At the bottom there." Her finger indicates a shadowy shape. "The fish store guy told me that rats are their biggest worry. He said I should put in the pipe so they'd have somewhere to hide. Then, if a rat goes after them, it'll get stuck in the pipe and drown."

Stella yanks her hand out of the water. "Ick. What do you do with the dead rat then?"

"That's the weirdest part." Aislyn cocks her head. "He said I don't have to take it out—the fish will eat it."

"No!" Stella frowns.

Aislyn nods absently. "Apparently they're omnivores."

"Really?"

Aislyn crooks her head at Stella, sees the lines of doubt on her high forehead, making her look childlike and innocent. In that moment she wants to reassure her friend that life will go on, love will come again, so she pokes a finger at her. "The things you don't know about goldfish, eh?" she says.

The sun's rays catch in the tight kinks of Stella's dark hair and Aislyn's eyes are drawn again to the reflection of sun in the peaks and troughs of those waves. Without realizing where she is going, she muses how those kinks might feel like coarse pubic hair beneath the tactile pads of her fingers. The thought halts her in mid-breath.

Aislyn rises from her crouch at the side of the pond and as she does, her right hand reaches for Stella's dark crown. When her fingers find the wiry hair, she feels Stella's head swivel in surprise. Aislyn shuts her eyes, concentrates on feeling the curls against her palm. Under that is the warmth and softness of her friend's scalp, the blood pulsing beneath a layer of skin.

Landing

Friday traffic along the Upper Levels Highway moves like a Hollywood police chase, cars swerving between lanes and passing Beth at warp speed. She stays in the slower right-hand lane as long as she can before rolling down her window to hand-signal a lane change. Her maroon Fairlane coughs into an opening in the middle lane but almost immediately she squints at the flash of quartz headlights in her rear-view mirror.

A huge SUV looms behind as she crests the hill into Horseshoe Bay and sees the lights of the small village glinting on the water below. Dusk is already hard upon the land and the last vestige of daylight is a strip of grey between the mountains and the falling night. She pumps the spongy brakes of the old Ford and coasts down the hill toward the ferry landing, the impatient SUV hovering on her bumper. At the delta of lanes feeding to the ticket booths, she slows for a speed bump and the SUV roars past.

She takes a hand off the steering wheel to rub at the tightness of her shoulders and neck as the old car creaks over the rise, then rocks onto the flat again. Her slow march toward the wall of ticket booths takes a full minute.

"Ferry's a half hour late," says the cashier, reaching for Beth's credit card.

Beth's grey eyes swing past the glass booth to the darkening horizon but no white ferry appears in the distance.

The cashier hands her a ticket. "Lane 77," she says.

Beth lifts her foot off the brake, allowing the sheer weight of the steel car to pull her down to the corral of waiting cars on the landing.

Slipping between two lanes dominated by hulking 4X4s, Beth puts the gearshift in PARK but leaves the noisy engine running. It has been cold and damp all day and she doesn't want to shut off the heater while she waits for the ferry. Outside, the night yawns like an empty cave and the darkness washes over her in a wave of exhaustion.

She shrugs her shoulders out of a navy overcoat that had once been her grandfather's, tugging at its worn collar to cover herself like a blanket. She peels off her toque and runs her hand through the cloud of curls freed from restraint, stuffs the hat between window and cheek, laying her head against the makeshift pillow.

It is all the noise and bluster, Beth thinks as she closes her eyes, the constant impatience of the city that always leaves her so drained. She wishes she could persuade her old parents to leave their west end condo and move up the coast where life is simpler and where it would be easier for her to help out. She is torn between wanting to be there for them and an overwhelming desire to tell them that she has a life of her own. Where was it written, Beth simmered behind the quieting curtain of closed eyelids, that women are meant to be the caretakers of an entire family system?

"Hello!" She hears the insistent voice behind the fog of her exhaustion. "Hello, hello!"

Cracking her eyelids, Beth sees the top half of a small boy, maybe three or four years old, leaning out the driver's window of the truck beside her, his round hand waving side to side in a mechanical motion.

Beth stares dumbly at the child, understanding slowly that his olive-skinned hand is waving at her. She presses her lips together, frowning to discourage his attention, then immediately sees what he must see, a tired and grumpy old woman.

The thought prods at her and so she mouths the word "Hello" and lifts her hand to wave back quickly. It is enough: the boy rewards her with a large smile before retreating, black eyes shining, into the truck's cab.

Beth sees the child curl himself against the truck's male driver. The man lifts an arm over the boy, laying his elbow on the sill of the open window and cupping his hand around the child's small shoulders. From somewhere outside the truck, light glints off the gold wedding band on his large-fingered hand. Beth stares sleepily at the ring and then at the black-haired knuckles of the man's hand stroking the child's downy head. The child leans back into the hand, fitting his crown to the shape of that palm and lying against the armour of chest that, Beth realizes now, must belong to Father.

The child settles as Beth's eyelids droop again and she shifts her shoulders to burrow into the driver's seat, looking for a more comfortable position. A few minutes later, she lets go, drifting into the foggy domain of pre-sleep until a sound from the truck startles her. Without moving from her reclined pose, she opens heavy eyelids on the father climbing from the truck's cab and shutting the door carefully. Immediately the small boy leans through the open window, and Beth can see the thick lashes of the child's big eyes watching Father's every move.

The man is ordinary-looking, thinning hair and slightly paunched gut. Nothing special, Beth decides as she watches him open the rear door. But she is struck by the way his large, hairy hands remove his leather jacket, holding the coat as though it was an infant and laying it gently, almost lovingly, on the back seat. He returns to the driver's door where the imploring reach of his son's outstretched arms makes him smile, and the man lifts the child through the window in a great hug. Father and son climb back into the front seat and, when the door shuts this time, Beth lifts her head, eyes opened wide, craning to peer into the truck's shadowy interior.

It is not until she feels the strain in her neck that Beth senses her voyeuristic behaviour. Embarrassed, she rests her head back against the side window and rolls further onto her left, her spine more definitely toward the truck. But something has shifted and the moment of quiet descent has vanished. For several minutes she lies staring at the press of cars around her, imagining other families tucked away inside the metal vehicles, the conversations and laughter and annoyances occurring inside each one of them, those predictable dynamics of family. Then she sighs and pulls her arm out from under the old coat to check her watch, wondering if what she feels in her gut is hunger.

6:00 p.m.: almost dinner time. She runs a veined hand across her tired forehead and yawns, stretching as she rolls back against the driver's seat. She fantasizes arriving home to a lit fire and the warm smells of dinner cooking, and then she makes a wry face, remembering the tired contents of her refrigerator—eggs, a sad lettuce, some bread—and the fact that there is nobody to cook for her. She sidesteps the latter thought and concentrates instead on the lack of food, but the mere idea of trying to create an appetizing meal from such sparse beginnings sends her back to searching the glistening harbour. In the deep blackness, a sparkle of lights signals the ferry's still-distant approach.

She rests a hand on her belly. A growing rumble there is uncomfortable, almost as though she is sickening with flu. But the thought is so neurotic that she rolls her head from side to side to shake off the idea. And now, in the corner of her eye, she catches sight of the little boy again.

He has crawled across his father to stretch his hand for the side view mirror, tilting it so he can see himself, then licking his finger and sliding the wet digit down the glass. He does this several times and then decides to lick his entire palm, slapping the mirror's surface with his damp imprint.

Beth watches the boy's game, fascinated by his absorbed dedication but distracted by a growing anticipation of the father's response. Father is turned away, conversing with an unseen passenger on the other side of the cab, totally unaware of the child's antics. Beth's expectation sits heavy in her belly and her breathing quickens until the child finishes his happy game of spitting and smearing and sits back against his father again.

Spent, the boy rests once more, and once more the man's thick fingers begin to stroke the boy's crown, face, neck. The child sits limply, soothed into a place of quiet contentment by Father's hands.

Beth's view is of the back of the child's head and she imagines that he has closed his eyes, perhaps inserted thumb in mouth as a gesture of complete surrender, the way her children had done decades before.

She feels again the weight of a child in her lap and remembers those quiet, slow moments when her children rested there, enfolded in her arms, doe-eyed and watching. Little monarchs in the seat of their country.

Watching the father's hand, she can feel the silky down of the child's hair beneath her own palm, the velvety smoothness of his skin against her rougher flesh, and the heat of that small body's temperature, its blood so much closer to the surface. The kinesthetic memories are hypnotizing and Beth succumbs to a perfect sense of calm, her breathing slowing to a steady rhythm. Then, from somewhere subterranean, a deep instinct rises and Beth gulps at the air, a fish sobbing out of water.

When the cars are loaded on the ferry, Beth is directed to the upper car deck and she loses sight of the truck with its dark-haired males. She sits in her old Ford and waits for the din of unloading passengers—their loud voices above the setting of car alarms and the repetitive thunk of door locks—to die. It is cold on the car deck but the startling light and noisy confusion of the upper passenger deck are too much for her, and she stays in the car instead. She watches the blackness slide past as the ferry leaves the harbour, tiny lights from distant island homes pricking the cape of night with gold.

Further out in the sound, the reflection of ferry lights on the ebony water makes her think how cold the ocean would be if ever the captain issued orders to abandon ship. She shivers at the darkness of the thought and then she wonders whether her naval officer father had ever held such dark fears. She sees the image of the younger man in the photo by her mother's bedside table and, from the caverns of childhood, another memory rises.

A summer's evening, fidgety and bored with nothing to do. Her presence so cloying that her mother sends her away, tells her to go find her sister or brother. And during that long walk down the hallway from the kitchen, a build of anticipation, of dread; the gnawing of some need welling up in her middle. She is maybe five years old, seeking some unidentifiable comfort, some concrete thing she cannot truly comprehend, and so, when she passes the open living-room door and sees the back of Father's head above the armchair, she hesitates only a second before dropping to her knees and crawling into the room. Silently she approaches his chair and sits on the floor behind him, and silently she pulls herself up to standing, reaching around to slap her hands over his eyes and yell, "Guess who?!"

And afterwards the rush of time, the rest of the memory blurred by his explosion. The painful grip where his hands grabbed her arms, the roaring throb of blood in her temples, the yells and confusion of others coming into the room to see what was wrong.

"Your father was in the war," her mother tried to soothe her later. "You must never, ever sneak up on him."

Yet even after the incident, as Beth came to call it, never, ever her father's lap for a throne. No apologetic hug or explanation; never his caressing hand on her head or hair, that protective hold of her small body.

The ferry disgorges its load of cars into the black night and Beth follows the snaking tail of headlights up the hill to the highway, driving home alone through the darkness. The dense forest looms on either side of the road, adding weight to the shadows in the yellow cone of her dim headlights, and she feels herself shrink into her body as she drives, preserving her energy and warmth as best she can.

To keep her deepening thoughts at bay, Beth considers what she will do when she arrives home. She will unpack the car, open a can of soup to heat and call her lover to let him know she's back.

"That's good," he will say, glad she is safely home.

Maybe then she will tell him about the small boy at the ferry terminal, his image still so strong with her that she would like to share that moment of time when the father's fingers had cupped his son's dark head like a crown. But as she imagines her description, Beth realizes her words will conjure an image only for herself; they will not convey to her lover what it is that she would like him to know.

She tries, then, to figure out exactly what it is she wants to say and her lover's face comes to mind as she thinks about how he listens to her, a look of consternation always on his brow as he tries to follow her disjointed thoughts. A concerned look that changes to another, softer look when they make love. And now she feels his touch, the way his large workman's hand slides beneath her head and cradles her neck as he tells her, "Let go, babe," dipping and riding above her, slowly at first, then faster, building the crescendo.

What she wants to tell him—what she is not sure how to communicate—is how glad she is for the fact of time. How knowing where to place things—memories, images, thoughts—on its continuum has kept her from landing somewhere she is not yet ready for. A shopping cart maybe, or worse.

I Don't Do Coy

Y ou probably learned about sex by watching the animals on
your farm in Wyoming (or wherever it was you said you were
from).

Not me. I learned about it in the cold, concrete basement of an elementary school, a building constructed expressly for the population created by all that wartime sex.

I imagine you hung over a fence while your father or uncle, some male relative, led the stallion into the corral. I picture the brood mare prancing skittishly, eyes rolled back in fury or anticipation. Who knows what mares feel as the stud approaches?

That grey-painted basement where we sat while the school nurse talked about our inevitable future was really the music room. Twice a week we filed down the narrow stairwell to fill the darkness in that room with songs from the turquoise-coloured *Songs for Canadian Schools*. And when we sang "Sweet Betsy from Pike" and "Underneath the Spreading Chestnut Tree," we were blissfully unaware of Betsy or Willy's sex life. If they even had one.

As you were likely unaware of the wind sweeping off the hills or the early leaves on the trees while the stallion mounted his mare. You were probably so focused on the thrust of his haunches that the weather didn't seem remarkable. But maybe it registered somewhere in your subconscious; maybe, years later, the gentle feel of a breeze on your cheek would bring it all back when you first lay naked with a woman.

We sat at the other end of the music room on the day we found out what would happen to us, ten-year-old girls with vague imaginings of future breasts and pubic hair. The school nurse herded us into the rows of cold, hard seats and we were nervous and flighty, like sheep before the shearing. We knew there was a movie—Teacher had already said— but only Shelley Ritchie, with long curly hair and matching eyelashes, knew why the boys weren't invited.

Shelley was the first of us to wear a bra, coming to school one day in a crisp, white blouse, through which the straps announced themselves like a red-circled spelling mistake.

"Shelley's an Early Bloomer," my mother said when I told her about it. I awaited some further explanation, but none came.

It was Shelley, though, in a girls-only huddle one rainy recess, who told us how, when we had our twelfth birthday, we would begin to bleed from an invisible place between our legs.

"So that babies can be made," she nodded with authority.

And you—when the stallion and bulls were put to stud, what explanation were you given about the female heat? Over the years you must have learned how to read the signs yourself, so you'd know when it was time to bring the two together. But I wonder if the mating season struck you as anything more than a practical fact: did you feel a sense of marvel at the cyclic nature of the seasons or were you aware only of a crucial sense of purpose, the timing of next year's young?

The developing stages of the female body on the movie screen reminded me of a page in our *World Book Encyclopedia,* drawings of mankind's progression from ape to upright being. But something—the why of it all, maybe—was missing.

Afterwards, after the nurse had demonstrated how to lock the tabs of a pad into the plastic ends of a sanitary belt, we were invited to ask questions.

"Don't feel shy, girls," she announced, hands clasped primly at her diaphragm. "Ask me anything you want to know."

I stared at the dark shadows of the room, still reeling from the 2-D images of dotted lines tracing the ovum's route down the fallopian tubes to the cozy nest of the prepared uterus.

What did you ask? Anything at all? Or was it perfectly clear that once the stallion dismounts, there is nothing more to be done? I bet it never crossed your mind, watching the rutting in the corral, to be embarrassed. It was only animal instinct: the male impregnates the female and if the female feels any violation, it is all in her head. Later, of course, it is all in her body.

In that darkened music room, Shelley Ritchie's hand rose determinedly, fingers waggling for Nurse to see. Only Shelley was matter-of-fact—brave—enough to ask for specifics.

"How does the boy egg get into the vagina?"

175

Shelley had already given us a lunch-hour synopsis of ejaculations. She'd described the male sperm, where it came from, even how to make it appear. Obviously Early Bloomers knew more than the rest of us.

"And you can't make babies with a man unless you're really in love with him," Shelley told us. "My mom said."

Shelley's mom's dictum seemed self-evident after the nurse's oblique answer about how the sperm got to the egg. We *yuck*ed and *grossed* over the details of intercourse for most of an afternoon, quivering with the impossibility of such an idea. Then we found the *Penthouse* in Mr. Ritchie's desk.

I wonder if that was how you were introduced to women? If the suggestive poses of centrefolds recalled for you the mare's heat? Maybe you knew, from watching the rut, the attainable heights of female fever. But how did you learn to ignite and stoke the fire of a woman's skin? When and where to alternate between roughness and gentleness? Technique doesn't come from observing the sweating, biting tons of muscle wrassling in a Wyoming corral.

By sixth grade, Shelley and I were reading the letters to the *Penthouse* editor out loud to each other.

"Listen to this," Shelley squealed one day. "This woman goes to the movies alone and just as the movie starts, some guy asks if he can sit beside her. 'He looked like a nice enough guy so, even though there were lots of empty seats in the theater, I said yes and he sat down beside me. After a few minutes, I felt his hand on my knee'!"

"Ewww!"

"Yeah! 'He leaned to ask if I minded and ...'—get this!—'I thought I should mind, but I didn't. I felt like I was under some kind of a spell and so, a little while later, when his hand began stroking my thigh, I leaned back against the chair and just enjoyed the feeling.' Can you imagine? What a whore!"

Is that what you called the girls who liked it? Did you talk about girls like Mary Anne Jervis, her huge tits bobbing beneath her sweater and her too-dark eyes simultaneously inviting and repulsing you, as though she were nothing but trash? Her urges the same as yours, but her sexual experiences making her a slut and you a mere conduit.

The man and the woman in the *Penthouse* letter missed the end of the movie. They left early and walked to her car, climbed into the back seat and pulled off their clothes. There, the woman wrote (and here Shelley sighed loudly), "I had the best sex of my life!"

Was your first lay in a car or in the hayloft with some city girl? Was it love, the kind Shelley's mom talked about, or pure animal lust?

I used to imagine meeting a stranger in the dark of a theatre. For years my fantasy spilled out of the theatre into a parking lot, my hunger growing until the idea of sex in the back seat of a car had taken on mystic proportions.

It gnawed at my imagination until long after my first sexual tangle was forgotten. Then I met you.

I like to make situations comfortable as soon as possible. I'm one of those people—maybe you don't know we exist—who assess any new environment by checking for emergency exits and getting the general feel of things before relaxing into the setting. For me, a new relationship develops linearly, progressing along a continuum like the ape-to-man and girl-to-woman scenario.

So when the front manager says, "Mae, this is Corbin. You'll both be in the box office tonight," I go into my comfort-making mode.

"Corbin," I stick my hand out. "Nice to meet you."

But you seem taken aback by that outstretched hand. I wonder, in the instant of your hesitation, if you're the kind who dislikes forthrightness, preferring coy women. Then your palm encircles my fingers and I'm inside the lasso of your grip.

Maybe I go too far with the comfort thing that night. But you're so quiet that I think you must be shy. So I ask lots of questions, hoping to put you at your ease. Maybe I'm wrong, though; maybe that's your style. Maybe you only act shy because you've learned it will draw others—women—to you.

(Is that what happened in the movie theatre? The man let the woman build on his groundwork?)

I notice your red leather boots and bright paisley shirt, but they do not alert me (as in retrospect I think they should have). I'm more interested in the threads you dangle like hints, incomplete answers about the world behind your flamboyant exterior.

"I've never heard that name before," I say after we're introduced.

"Celtic." An indifferent shrug signifies you've done this before, explaining yourself and your past.

My imagination leaps at a sudden chain of associations: Celtic—Druids—rituals.

I step right into the corral then, asking, "Where are you from?" Assuming somewhere exotic. Ireland. Wales. The Isle of Man.

You turn to look straight at me, the first time I've had a chance to study the graceful line of your nose, the fine square of your chin. Yours is a delicate face, finely etched like the faery faces of childhood picture books.

"Actually I'm from the States. Wyoming."

And I laugh, tilting my head back in reaction to my own naïveté and a desire to make so much from so little. I'm almost aware, as I laugh, of your green eyes watching me with interest.

When I try to explain my amusement, you continue to watch with intent. There is more than curiosity—enchantment, maybe—in your look.

"I thought," my hand waves explanatorily, "you know—that with a Celtic name you must be from overseas."

You nod in response, still openly staring, and then your lips move: "You have a lovely smile." The words hang before me, so unconscious, so tantalizing, that I hold my breath, waiting for ... an explanation? An apology?

Because I do not know what to do with your offering. You have laid this thing at my feet, left it there by itself, and I do not know what to do.

"Thank you," I mumble.

A whisper of a smile dances round your eyes and mouth, and I respond by smiling again, this time not so broadly, and then I turn to business. I look through the grate of the box-office window, checking to see whether anyone wants a ticket. They don't.

I am glad you seem more at ease. But there is something else now; something new at work here.

Much later I will think I should have understood that your noisy shirt and loud boots are not the clothes of a shy person. Especially the green sports jacket, its mossy reflection in your eyes a kind of camouflage—how much of an effect were you aware of making?

For half an hour we sit in profile to each other, facing the metal bars of the box-office window and exchanging tickets for money. In the next lull it is you who begins the conversation.

"Do you know someone in the show?"

"My daughter's in the chorus."

You nod pensively. "My brother-in-law has a solo."

This is when I might have turned away, gone back to sorting tickets and cash. But you cock your head at me and your green eyes challenge with a hot mirth that both suggests and invites.

My eyes drift away from your green ones and rest on the dip and wave of your blond curls. Brother-in-law, I repeat in my head.

"Your daughter's musical?"

"Yes," I assert, imagining your fair hair encircled by a wreath as you dance, naked and sweating, at the Beltane fires. "She plays a fiddle"—I look at your green eyes again—"and the bodhran." A flicker of firelight behind the mossy banks of green. The Beltane orgy so clearly conjured that I blush and turn away. But when I look back, the heat of invitation is still there.

"The bodhran?" You sound amused. "How long?"

I want to lie on those hills of moss, feel their soft cushioning beneath my naked skin; close my eyes against the delicate light of the solstice while faeries dance in woodland rings and you dance above me. But now a net drops and I feel its constriction. I sit very still, frozen in silence.

Without any more preparation, the relationship begins.

When the box office closes, we total the cash in silent computation, then lock the money away to go watch the show. I push quietly on the heavy doors to the theatre, the light from the lobby throwing a momentary spotlight on us as we enter. A white-haired couple at the back of the theatre turns with ferocious frowns and, standing there beside you, I feel as though we've been caught at something.

You take my elbow as though we're a couple, point at a section of empty rows on the side, steer me towards them. I settle into a seat, too aware of your closeness and almost forgetting why we're here.

On stage the set is scant, graduated black boxes placed strategically for various solos. A chunky man in a green robe steps onto one now.

I feel the pressure of your elbow as you lean into me.

"That's my brother-in-law."

Brother-in-law, I remember. Marriage, I think.

From atop his perch, your brother-in-law—The Lord High Executioner—launches into a throaty baritone. His solo is punctuated by melodramatic expressions: the exaggerated black lines of his make-up and the thrusts of a glinting sword.

On the armrest between us, your elbow touches mine as we applaud. Its warmth distracts me as the girls' chorus trips onto the stage.

My daughter laughs and steps in choreographed sequence with the others. But the lighting is unprofessional, and the girls' shadows loom eerily large, making them more satanic than innocent.

"Which one's your daughter?" you whisper, so close to my ear that tiny droplets of condensation remain after the scald of breath.

I point at the stage—a senseless gesture—and turn to speak directly into your ear, "The red hair."

When you nod, I feel the tickle of your hair against my nose and I sit back, pull quickly into myself. The idea occurs to me that I'm not enjoying my child's performance so much as my own. I concentrate, drift slowly into the story on stage, watching my flesh and blood as her head tips in bashful pleasure and her kimono swishes in mock humility. I watch with the strange sensation that she is much better than I at doing coy. And then you are back at my ear, pressing me with another potion.

"Very graceful."

With your breath so near again, I wonder what I'm supposed to do, my body thrust so close to yours. Without pulling my head away, I nod in the dark, electrified by the almost negligible touch of our hands on the armrest. I wonder, as a charge races up my arm and across my chest, piercing my nipples, why you don't move your hand. Can you feel it or is it only my wily hormones running amok?

In the denseness of the theatre, you turn towards me and I feel, rather than see, your smile. When I face you, the light on your pale brow and blond curls play tricks on me. A shadow flickers in your eyes, maybe the reflection of a spotlight on stage or maybe the lights from another fire, and I don't know any longer what is real, what is lighting, what is theatre.

Many years later I will be told that the word *mikado* means "majestic opening." But tonight I do not know that. Tonight I try denial.

My sensibilities are fuzzy, oscillating between the effects of your drama and those of the actors we have come to watch. I listen to the chorus but am distracted by the tickle of your wool pants against the bare skin of my leg.

On stage I watch the Mikado strut and bellow but it is the warm cup of your palm on my kneecap that grabs my attention. And when Nanki-Poo and Yum-Yum launch into "Were You Not to Ko-Ko Plighted," I am gone, senseless to anything but the increasing pressure of your thigh.

I close my eyes as your fingers glide up my leg and the blood explodes in my centre. Words slide across the back of my eyelids like a line of breaking news at the bottom of a television screen: *Wyoming. Celtic. Brother-in-law.* I wait for more, for words like marriage or wife, but my imagination is in overtime: *pagan, Druid, ritual.*

When the lights rise at the end of Act I, your arm lies across my left thigh, your thumb in the fold between right leg and pubic mound. I avoid your eyes as we stand but feel your hand move against the small of my back, steering me towards the exit.

The front manager finds us in the lobby, a bouquet of roses in his hand. He holds the cone of flowers out to you.

"For Pity Sing," he says, and you take them into your arms like a newborn babe, heading backstage with the delivery.

I watch you go and for the first time since meeting you, I am alone and clear-headed.

Heat

When she bought the big house on the hill, Marnie hoped Guy would go in on it with her, sell his own place as a gesture of solidarity and commitment. But though he shares the new house, Guy has made no move to sell his own. Instead, he uses it as a refuge whenever they argue—frequently these past months—threatening by running away for an afternoon or a day. He never stays gone long: the fridge and hot water at his place are shut off and the food supply is limited to canned soup.

They've been together nearly five years, but lately things have come to a point where sometimes Marnie eggs Guy on in order to have the quiet hillside to herself, whole days undisturbed by his mess or noise. If the new property was more manageable, she would tell him to move back to his own place for a while. But the repairs and maintenance of an acreage seem never-ending and the huge garden takes more time and energy than Marnie has to spare. Often, now, she thinks back to her tiny house by the sea and wonders whether it was a mistake to trade for this spacious but heavy burden.

Tonight she sits alone in the open living room as darkness descends. She does not turn on the lights but stares out the windows at the falling night, waiting. When the first flash from the lighthouse across the water bursts into the room, she watches its beam of light travel the shadowy length of the interior walls. She waits, and when it comes again, there is a small blip before the larger flash, a rhythm similar to her heartbeat, the faint thump followed by a more definite one. That small detail provides a flicker of hope against a lurking threat of despair.

During Marnie's last fall in the house by the sea, Gena had called twice from the city. The first was her annual birthday call and the second was to ask if Marnie would keep an eye on the local real estate market, find her some waterfront.

Marnie asked for parameters—price, size, location—and the answer was a surprise: "I want what you have."

She had sounded almost desperate, her voice an uncharacteristic simper, and the sound made Marnie's shoulders lift in tension.

"... somewhere right beside the water so I can hear the waves," Gena's plea continued.

Marnie had turned to stare out the window at the sea beyond. The waves that day were battleship grey, their white tops muddied with the lifting and churning of sand and kelp, bits of wood torn from log booms. Though they were threatening, they were also hypnotically settling. Marnie felt herself slip into the push and pull of the tide as it crashed at the breakwater in front of her. She shivered at a sudden chill and wrapped her free arm around herself in a protective hug.

She waited a week before calling a real estate agent she knew.

"How flush is your friend?" the agent asked.

"Shaughnessy," said Marnie.

"Okay," he responded happily.

Within days he phoned back. "There's a place," he said, "with an older house about a mile down the beach from you. Level waterfront with a berm between it and the highway, so it's quiet."

Gena didn't bat an eyelid at the exorbitant price. She and Brad planned to paint and do some minor repairs, use the place for weekend getaways. When she couldn't find a contractor to do the work, Marnie mentioned the possibility to Guy.

"Why not?" he asked at her hesitancy.

Marnie shrugged. "Friends and business. You know."

But Guy was happy to have the work and Gena was happy to have someone she could work with.

"I'm pretty good at reading people, you know," she told Marnie. "I can tell you two things about that man: he loves you and he's a good guy." Then she laughed and leaned forward to touch Marnie's elbow, give her an exaggerated wink.

Guy puts in seven and a half hours on a building site and then comes home for a shower and drops into his La-z-Boy until dinner. He cooks on weekends, whipping up a stir-fry or barbecuing hamburgers, but during the week he is too tired to do more than open a can of soup or heat junk food.

As the week progresses, the house accumulates a layer of dust and dirt, various piles of stuff needing to be put away or dealt with. When Marnie reaches her limit—a limit undefined except by a growing testiness that makes Guy turn away or parry with escalating defensiveness—she barks at him.

"Can't you help out a little? Wash the floors or something?"

He peers at her over top of the tortoise-shell eyeglasses he wears for reading. They're Marnie's glasses—too small for his face—but he won't go to the doctor about his weakening vision. He looks slightly ridiculous, especially trying to be the sane one now.

"The house isn't dirty, Marn. Let it go."

She has tried to tell him about the perfect peace she envisions, a state she believes would evolve naturally from more downtime, less busyness. Somewhere inside she can feel the existence of a calm serenity, the state of grace she aspires to.

But there's no point in trying to talk to Guy about that. They've been down this road before and he does not understand her desire for an alternate existence.

"That's woo-woo stuff," he says whenever she brings it up. He holds his index fingers like antennae on the side of his head and sings the *Outer Limits* theme song—*doo* doo doo do, *doo* doo doo do.

"Guy, I'm drowning!" she wails this evening. "It may be only an illusion, but I need the house to be clean!"

"You don't need anything, Marnie. You have a home, food, friends. What else could you want?"

"Some relief!" she snaps.

For over a year, Gena's building site has been a topic of discussion with the locals. Feeling partly responsible for what has become the town's first monster home, Marnie winces when people make snide remarks about the number of times the painters'—or electricians' or plumbers'—trucks are parked out front of "The House that Never Ends." Some of the tradesmen tell her scornful stories about either Brad or Gena and Marnie dutifully carries the gossip home to Guy. She tells him with a sense of self-righteousness, but as soon as the malicious gossip is out of her mouth, she regrets her lack of control.

Gena has been pressing Marnie for a month to come view her masterpiece. Today, returning from the tour, Marnie carries a vision of the cathedral-ceilinged living room in muted colours, huge cedar beams echoing the trees outside. Gena had linked arms to walk her onto the deck and admire their private stretch of beach and Marnie had pictured Brad and Gena there, raising crystal goblets of the best champagne to the sinking sun, then wandering back inside the exquisite residence, calling the maid for hors d'oeuvres.

She tells Guy about the tightness she'd felt in her chest at Gena's, a tension like the set spring of the rat trap in the greenhouse.

Guy stares at her in curiosity. "Are you jealous?" he asks. "You wish you had that kind of money?"

Marnie opens the fridge door, busies herself with unpacking groceries.

"Money doesn't buy happiness, Marn," he says from across the room.

She puts the butter in the dairy compartment and lets the plastic door bang shut. The noise makes her jump, reminds her how, when Guy tested the rat trap, her heart had hiccupped in response to the snapping jaw. Then, like now, she saw how life threatened to kill her.

Whenever Guy highlights her flaws, Marnie reacts to his disapproval with a sense of shame. Admitting her envy for Gena's house had put her there again, wrapped in a shroud of unworthiness. Wanting to hide from the sense of failure, Marnie filled the bathtub and added a heavy dose of lavender oil.

Soaking in the water, she takes its heat into her bones and tries to forget about the ongoing struggle with Guy. Their head-butting always revolves around whose approach to life is better and it's hard to ignore the fact that Guy is a happier person. But the constant arguing has made Marnie reconsider the benefits of being single; of being miserable by herself.

She lifts a pink arm outside the tub, reaches for the floor. Her hand finds the newspaper and water drips off her so that when she lifts a section, she has to peel at the edge to turn the page. She checks the *For Rent* column, but there are only two houses listed and neither allows pets. She thinks about being petless too, remembering the bliss of quiet that comes only with utter solitude. Then she sighs and turns back to the horoscope page.

Under *Libra* it says her Venus, Mars and Mercury are on top of each other, pressed so close together that there is no room to move. "All that constant pushing makes for a very fussy personality. You need to sit still. Wait and listen."

Marnie stares at the last line and wonders how it could be possible to sit still in her life. She shuts the paper and drops it on the floor, closes her eyes.

Sometimes, now, she finds herself back where she's been before, stalled at some kind of crossroads and repeating wrong turns. At night, in the dark of the bedroom, she talks to herself, trying to control—or reaffirm—the flame within.

You're not a bad person, she whispers. *You just need to make some changes.*

So she thinks about leaving.

Guy has always said that what he loves about Marnie is her preference for solitude; the way she doesn't need to socialize all the time like Ellen, his last girlfriend.

Ellen had once coerced Guy into stopping somewhere on their way home from work. He had been dirty and tired, just wanting to go home to a shower and dinner, but Ellen insisted she needed his help to lift a box at work. She was a municipal employee and Guy grumbled that surely they could find another flunky. It was a dark and cold November evening, and when they opened the doors at the community centre, the sudden splash of light was blinding.

"Surprise!" A huge chorus roared at him and then he noticed the fluttering birthday banners.

Early in their relationship Guy had warned Marnie: "Don't ever throw me a surprise party." She looked up at his 6'2" height, saw his hazel eyes blazing with sincerity, so she nodded in sombre agreement. At the same time she'd felt a slight breathlessness that he was already assuming a future together, but then she remembered Allan, her former husband. Allan who might have said the same thing—"Don't throw me a surprise party"—but meant the complete opposite.

Still, when Marnie suggests a celebration for Guy's fiftieth, she isn't surprised by his response.

"A party? No thanks."

What does surprise her is his rescue of the idea a few weeks later.

"Let's have the bonfire on my birthday, invite a few friends."

For Marnie, bonfire day is sacrosanct, a day as holy as Christmas to others. For this one day each year she allows herself to relax, let go of the real world and sink into a few quiet hours of reflection. But Guy's suggestion paints a whole different scenario.

She sees him sit up in excitement and her heart sinks. Though Guy avoids most social gatherings, he loves attention and the current gleam in his eyes tells her that the idea has already taken root; it's too late to change direction. This year she will have to put on the ritz and play hostess, bustling about and winding herself as tight as a slingshot for people she doesn't know, has never even met. Worse, if they're like Guy at social functions, talking only about themselves and drinking more than they should, ignoring her glass when they refill their own, the day will be full of pretense.

In the bath Marnie thinks how it hasn't mattered until now that the two of them have no mutual friends. Guy has always presented himself as a loner, practically a hermit. Only recently has Marnie met his brothers, men who live less than five minutes away but who Guy had never thought to introduce her to. After wondering a long while whether that omission was out of ignorance or shame, she had finally asked. Guy seemed genuinely bewildered by the question and stared at her in surprise: "Do you want to meet them?"

Tonight Guy opens the bathroom door and pokes his head into the steamy room to read the names of a tentative guest list. Marnie shudders, imagining all the people she's heard about for years. She wonders what—or if—Ron and Cheryl, Stu and Maggie have heard about her. And then she wonders what she's really doing with someone like Guy, rough-and-tumble and so easygoing next to her determined drive for perfection.

She lifts a hand to her brow as though shading herself from the overhead light. When she exhales, the sigh that escapes feels as though it has travelled a long distance from her centre.

"Sure," she responds when he finishes the list. "Sounds good."

The bonfire is their final thrust at the approach of winter. Every November they heave pruned boughs and windfall onto the huge pile of cuttings collected from Marnie's farm-sized garden. Guy pokes a torch at the heap and the flames build slowly, tickling the outdoor whisper of cold.

The day is so removed from her normally overstuffed schedule that Marnie spends the first hour fidgeting, feeling an underlying guilt at her idleness. Instead of directing a class of crazed ten-year-olds or trying to check off a list of things to pick up/drop off/clean/fix/buy, the day is as empty as a midsummer sky and she shuttles back and forth to the house for snacks or another sweater. When finally she recognizes the source of her anxiety, Marnie places one of the green plastic chairs front and centre at the bonfire and concentrates on the flames.

Guy sharpens roasting sticks and rakes at escaped embers, controlling the burn while Marnie perches on the circumference, staring at the heart of redness. The dogs lie nearby, jowls on paws, and even in grey, drizzly weather, the day becomes like a summer picnic: hours of rambling thoughts and afternoon daydreams. In front of the heat, everything slips away and Marnie feels herself unlock, a flower in bud.

Eventually the fire lies subdued in a tangle of glowing ash and she huddles closer in her chair. But when Guy again rakes in the embers, the flames shoot towards the sky with a venous burst of renewed energy and once more Marnie carries the chair away from the heat. When her face and shins become too hot, she turns her back to the fire, letting the heat massage her spine. And as the afternoon wanes, Marnie raises her eyes in the gathering darkness, watching the sparks lifting into the sky.

For Guy, relief is stepping through the door and kicking off his shoes at the end of a physically draining day, groaning with pleasure at the freeing of his tired feet. Marnie flinches at the thunk of his deep-treaded workboots, hearing the release of stones and dirt skittering across the floor. If she chides him, he does one of two things: rolls his eyes and skulks—sometimes stomps—to the darkness of the den and his computer. Or he turns on her like a dog protecting his food, growling to back her off.

In the past year Marnie has tried to change her approach to the chaos of the house, to see it as proof of their shared existence. For several months she practised noticing and then circling the rotten patches on the stairwell; ducking her head to avoid the dripping gutter as she unlocked the door. Inside, she accepted the scattered evidence of Guy's presence: misspelled lists of job supplies forgotten on the hall table, car trader magazines with Post-it-marked pages dropped beside his La-z-Boy, a mud-splashed thermal carafe on the kitchen counter, the grit on its base scratching as she slides it towards the sink.

But one night Marnie gets up from the couch, sees her new black pants covered in dog hair and the heat flares.

"Can't you at least keep the fucking dogs out of the living room?"

"Oh, for Christ's sake," Guy spikes back. "Do you want dogs or do you want a nicky-picky house!"

Her eyes fill as she leaves the room. In the bathroom she sits on the edge of the tub, her breath a stuttering of sobs as she watches the flow of water through a blur of tears.

Gena calls to tell her about the progress of her house.

"I'm so sick of looking at tiles and wallpaper and paint!" she groans.

"Poor you!" Marnie tries to sound sympathetic.

Gena has been a buddy since childhood, sharing birthday parties and sleepovers, developing breasts and starting her period with Marnie. At the height of adolescence, though, Gena's parents sent her to boarding school.

Marnie was still included whenever Gena's new friends arrived in their Fiats and BMWs, but after a while she felt like an outsider. It was not merely a lack of flashy clothes and money, but more the others' conversations about Capetown or Bali or the Yacht Club Christmas ball, places well beyond Marnie's experience.

When Gena married shortly after high school, she had kids right away. In a matter of years, the two friends drifted apart. Then, in her mid-twenties, Marnie and her new husband moved to a tiny post-war bungalow on the outskirts of Shaughnessy, near Gena's heritage house.

The two friends might have resumed a friendship then, but for Allan. At a dinner party, taking an instant dislike to Gena's husband, he refused to socialize with the Dexters again.

"It was like mixing champagne with beer," Allan said. "And we were the beer."

Marnie, too, had felt out of place in a room full of diamond- and gold-bedecked guests, but afterwards she saw it as her own under-confidence; nothing to do with Gena.

When the marriage to Allan failed, Marnie left the city for a job on the coast. She bought the small house on a remote stretch of water-front and the constantly changing moods and colours of the sea helped her relinquish the city life. For the first time she revelled in solitude, enjoying the remove of family and friends and finding solace in her aloneness.

Then, out of the blue, Gena called to wish her a happy birthday one fall, fanning the glow of memory. On a whim, Marnie invited Gena for a visit and the two reconnected as though there had been no hiatus. They began to meet every few months, at the seaside or in the city, and over lunch they talked about the past, rekindling memories of life in the time of Vietnam, JFK, flower power, the Pill. Though Gena had stayed clear of the psychedelic drugs and music on which Marnie had floated for years, something about being witness to those times—the sudden tumult of life around them and the way they'd been rocket-launched into adulthood without any preparation for such freedom—made both of them shiver in common remembrance. Looking back from the tre-mendous distance of their age, it seemed miraculous they'd survived those years at all.

At times, returning from the city to her tiny house, Marnie would feel an acute emptiness. Especially in the dark of winter or if the sea was stormy, the images of those laughing visits with Gena were like the waning glow of embers in her woodstove, waiting to be stoked.

Marnie wanted to ask if Gena was happy, if the fire still smouldered between her and Brad. But the gap between their present lives was still so great that the two friends spent little time there. It was safer to stay in the past.

Guy was forty-four to Marnie's forty-nine when they met. When he wondered about her single state, she tried to explain with words and chronological lists of events, describing the marriage to Allan and mentioning some recent lovers.

"But nobody of any substance." She shook her head, then immediately backpedalled. "Which is not to demean them. Just they didn't"— she shrugged—"understand me, I guess."

"You're sensitive," Guy responded. He nodded in what Marnie thought was either acceptance or reassurance.

She began to picture them sitting around the fireplace at night, laughing and drinking tea together. But first she tested him: "I have high expectations," she insisted. "I need a lot of support." Sufficient warning, she thought, to screen out another Allan.

Marnie can no longer remember what Guy answered, only that he wrapped his long arms around her as though sealing an agreement. In those days he was more physical, more tender in a rough sort of way.

Now he says things like, "Would I still be here if I didn't care?" and Marnie wonders why he asks *her* the question. When he's really angry, he uses her past as ammunition, lobbing grenades that would incinerate the blackest enemy. "The reason you're not married anymore is you're too damned hard to please," he accuses. "All those impossible demands."

After Gena bought her piece of oceanfront, Guy tried to persuade Marnie away from the beach. The influx of city buyers was fuelling a real estate boom and prices were climbing at alarming rates. "They're not making more waterfront," he said. "Sell."

Out the window she could see several building projects at various stages of completion. The new construction meant increased traffic and the highway had become a constant din of sirens, motorcycles and jake brakes. The quiet life she'd found here was gone now, the only silence in the middle of the night when hot flashes woke her.

The idea of another winter with two big dogs and a gangly man in her small house squeezed at Marnie. The alternative was to move into Guy's place, an oeuvre being hand-finished at his own personal pace.

But living in a construction zone, even under the guise of being in love, was so unattractive that Marnie called the real estate agent again.

He took her to the hillside house on a long shot. With the open view of the sea on one side and the expanse of acreage on the other, Marnie felt her Libran scales shift. Telling herself that perhaps the whisper of forest could replace the soothing sound of waves, she exchanged the noisy highway for the peaceful panorama of Georgia Strait. And in the blue distance, the picture-postcard view of the last manned lighthouse on the west coast.

"Oh, Marn!" Gena wailed. "I can't believe I'm finally going to be this close to you and now you're moving!"

But growing plans for her new property soon overrode the regret. Packing for her move, Marnie felt both guilty and relieved that she had an excuse to avoid Gena's constant updates.

After he has twenty names on the guest list, Guy stops. "That's it," he says. "I can't sleep more than ten couples at my house."

From across the kitchen, Marnie frowns in confusion.

He lifts his hands explanatorily. "Well, they're coming up from the city—they have to stay overnight."

Marnie concedes they can't drink beer all afternoon and drive home safely. But a week later, she overhears him on the phone.

"Okay, Ron. So you'll be on the 5:30 or the 7:30 ferry ..."

She stops chopping vegetables and the skin around her mouth tightens perceptibly.

When he hangs up she asks, "How long is the party going to last?" She lifts her brow, tries to make the question sound as though she's just wondering.

He gives her a disgusted look. "Are you trying to put a curfew on us?"

"If they come on the 7:30 they won't be here until 9:00. That sounds like an all-nighter."

"And?"

"I thought we were having a party, not a drunk."

"It's my fiftieth birthday, for Chrissakes. I'm not going to invite all

these people up here and then tell them we have to stop partying because Marnie doesn't want to be kept awake all night."

"So I should find somewhere else to sleep, then?"

"Maybe you should."

She lies on the bed, concentrating on her breathing. When she identi-
fies the reason for her anger—Guy telling her how to live in her own
house—she gets up and goes to the den.

She stands and listens outside the closed door. The lights are off and
there are none of the bleeping noises from his computer games.

Tapping lightly, she calls, "Guy?"

Nothing.

She pushes on the door. Its corner sticks against the frame and she
leans with her shoulder. The door swings open to the room.

In the dim light of the uncurtained window, Marnie sees that Guy
has unfolded the sofabed and lies like a child, curled foetally with his
mouth open. The lines of worry and frustration on his brow are relaxed and he looks less harried, less tired. She recalls an image of him
from their early days and wonders how sharing a home has somehow
managed to make loving him less fun. Wasn't it supposed to be the
other way around?

She hesitates in the doorway, the ghostly blue of his computer screen
showering the darkened room. Then she sighs and turns to leave.

"Marn?" His voice soft with sleep.

"Are you awake?"

He lifts his covers to invite her in. "C'mere."

She hesitates, then slips into his cave, glad for the warmth.

Marnie's current anxiety is as much about Gena and her damned house
as it is about Guy. Months after Gena hired him—months during
which Guy's mood fluctuated wildly with the ever-changing renova-
tions—Gena upped the ante to include a major addition to the existing
house, expanding the blueprints yet again. Three times the building

department had refused to permit her cantilevered monster, and one night Guy arrives home flummoxed by more changes.

"They want to scrap the reno." He looks exhausted. "They're going to tear it down, rebuild completely."

"Isn't that easier than a reno?"

He shakes his head despondently. "I'm a one-man band. The job's too big."

"You built your own place," Marnie encourages. "This would give you great referrals."

By the time the phone rings after dinner, Guy is calmer. Marnie hears him answer the call and slip, unawares, into his business voice.

Gena, she realizes. And then she hears him swear.

Marnie waits, listening to the silence from the other room. She stops folding laundry and pads across to the kitchen.

Guy's face like a stunned deer. When he sees her, the eruption begins.

"Your *friend*—" he spits "—is hiring Delamont. Wants me to work for the prick."

Marnie feels a chill of recognition. Behind the anger, Guy's palpable hurt.

"I wouldn't work for that fuck if he paid triple time!"

Later in the dark of the bedroom, he tells her how Gena's tone had been so reserved, so formal.

"Rehearsed—" Marnie guesses "—so there'd be no argument when she announced her one-eighty."

"*But Delamont's willing to hire you*," Guy mimics a smarmy voice. "*Phone him.*"

George Delamont, the small town's big-time contractor, often accused of having no ethics. Rumours raged about how he bribed council members or offered "incentives" to building inspectors, his forte the manipulation of local bylaws to accommodate controversial plans.

"As if," Guy coughs.

"Is Guy all right?" Gena calls a week later.

Marnie keeps her voice flat. "He's fine."

"Good. Because I don't want him to think I don't like him. But I need to get this house built. I need to be there. By the sea."

Marnie turns to stare at the lighthouse on its island. Soon, she thinks in the darkness of the afternoon. Soon the keeper will turn on the beam for the lost and foundering.

As she waits for the light, she thinks of all the things she wants to say to Gena, all the things she's imagined during the past week. After all, they are friends, friends who should be able to talk—and listen—to each other.

Her hand clutches the receiver. Words roll around in her head. Beneath her ribs the urge to speak like boiling reflux. Marnie opens her mouth, her tongue sticky with dryness. "Listen, Gena ..."

And Gena jumps in: "You know what I mean, don't you, Marn?" Her tone austere, just a hint of a dare.

Marnie gropes for control. She takes a breath and tries to regroup, but her timing is lost. The words have gone, flown like fading sparks, and slowly her mouth closes, lips sliding over teeth set firmly and finally together. Across the falling dusk comes the blinding flash of the lighthouse and, like a child swayed by candy, Marnie follows the beam's retreat, eyes wide open.

"Marn?" Gena says.

The light disappears and Marnie comes back to the call. "But how did you choose Delamont, Gena?" She hears the exasperated whine in her voice and recognizes the weak attempt to sidestep confrontation. The awareness makes her angry and she musters her determination, digging deep to fan the intention. But even as she does, Marnie feels a cooling sigh escape her lips.

"He's two houses over," Gena explains. "We invited him and his wife for drinks and we were complaining about the hard time we're having getting a permit. He offered to help."

The scene was so clear, so perfect: the two wives with their wine, Brad and Delamont with single malt Scotch, bellies sagging over Gucci belts. Talking local politics and how to get what Brad and Gena wanted from the still-innocent planners of a small-town board. Delamont, or maybe Brad, voicing doubts about Guy being the right person to get the job done; whether he even knew how to work the system.

As the day of the bonfire approaches, Marnie's regret deepens, the ritual simplicity of their winter event tarnished by Guy's plans to turn it into an extraordinary gala. Though she makes lists of things needed for the big day, Marnie wishes she'd ignored the milestone aspect of Guy's birthday, never suggested its celebration.

Two nights before the party, Guy answers the phone and Marnie hears him say, "Sure, come Friday night—it'll be a weekender."

She leaves the room, feeling her way along the unlit hallway. In the bathroom she kneels beside the tub, testing the water and increasing the flow of hot until steam billows into the air. When the temperature nears scalding, she stands and locks the door.

As she undresses, Marnie takes deep gulps of air, willing herself to focus on climbing into the heat and dissolving the residual tension of her body, all the angst she feels over the party and guests to come. Naked, she slips first one foot and then the other into the hot water, gasping at each new shock.

Lowering the rest of her body, Marnie grits her teeth as the heat envelops her. She closes her eyes and, after a while, pink and sweating, she submerges her face and head beneath the water's surface, looking up at the mist-dampened ceiling through the wavy medium of water. Here, now, she can see more clearly.

She thinks of Gena then, for some reason. Thinks how her handling of Guy was so harsh, so cold and unfeeling. But beneath Marnie's distress for Guy there had also been also an inkling of empathy for Gena. An understanding of how Guy can be such a letdown; how his lack of responsibility has frequently made Marnie feel like giving up on him.

The water is so hot she can feel herself cooking, her skin changing from its usual paleness to the colour of deep sunburn. The tightness in her shoulders relaxes and she gives in to the heat.

Behind her eyelids she sees the faces of Gena, Brad and Guy in the empty kitchen of Gena's new property. Such an auspicious beginning